Praise for SHERI REYNOLDS

"Ms. Reynolds's poetic gifts are uncommonly powerful."
—*The New York Times*

"Reynolds is a wonderful storyteller and master of pastoral imagery."
—*The New York Times Book Review*

"Reynolds . . . is a gifted writer with a deceptively simple style
and a keen ear for dialogue." —*The Boston Globe*

"Reynolds is the newest and most exciting voice to emerge in
contemporary southern fiction." —*San Francisco Bay Guardian*

"An imaginative tour de force . . . Pushing beyond the boundaries of her earlier work, Ms. Reynolds has created a life-affirming
novel that gathers the joy and pain of living into a celebration of
what it means to be human."

—*Richmond Times-Dispatch*, for *A Gracious Plenty*

A Gracious PLENTY

Also By SHERI REYNOLDS

Bitterroot Landing

The Rapture of Canaan

Firefly Cloak

The Sweet In-Between

The Homespun Wisdom of Myrtle T. Cribb

A Gracious PLENTY

SHERI REYNOLDS

TURNER

Turner Publishing Company

200 4th Avenue North • Suite 950 Nashville, Tennessee 37219

445 Park Avenue • 9th Floor New York, NY 10022

www.turnerpublishing.com

Cover design by Beth Middleworth

Book design by Glen Edelstein

Library of Congress Cataloging-in-Publication Data

Reynolds, Sheri.
 A gracious plenty / Sheri Reynolds.
     p. cm.
 ISBN 978-1-61858-031-3
 1. Burns and scalds--Patients--Fiction. 2. Dead--Miscellanea--Fiction.
 3. Psychological fiction. I. Title.
 PS3568.E8975G72 2012
 813'.54--dc23
                                   2012023039

For AMY LIANN TUDOR

Acknowledgments

THANKS TO MY BUDDIES—Amy Tudor, Allyson Rainer, Glen Turner, Dave Hendrickson, Lori Hamilton, Leaf Seligman, and Elizabeth Mills—for editorial advice, support, and friendship.

Thanks to Grandma Mary, Angeline, Aunt Dora, and Uncle James for teaching me about burns.

Thanks to my sweet family—to my Mamma, Daddy, Grandma, Genie, Chris, Caroline, Sammie, Jimmy, Paul, Mary Beth, Granny Gladys, Robert, Wanda, Glenn, Michelle, Julianne, and Granny Mary Jane.

Thanks to my new editor, Shaye Areheart, who believed in this book, and especially to my agent, Candice Fuhrman, who always did.

A Gracious PLENTY

A IN'T YOU GOT NO RESPECT for the Dead?" I holler. "Get outta here. Ain't you got no shame?"

But I'm wasting my breath. The children are running before I open my mouth, squealing and hightailing it around tombstones and trees, racing for the edge of the cemetery. A boy without a shirt dusts his belly on the ground and scrapes his back wiggling fast beneath the fence.

"You hateful old witch," he cries, but not until he's in the shrubbery on the other side. "You damn-fool witch."

I raise my stick and shake it at him.

By the time I get to the plot where they were playing, all that's left is a striped tank top and a bottle half-full of soda that they were throwing like a ball. They've cracked the plastic, and the liquid drizzles out dark. Fizz runs down my arm as I pick it up.

I apologize to Sarah Andrews Barfield, 1897—1949, and wipe the soda off her dingy stone with that child's shirt. It doesn't look like rain. Ants will come.

I stuff the shirt through the hole in the fence and then find a brick and a few fallen limbs to block off the space until I can get it patched.

On the way back to the house, I stop to visit with Ma and

Papa for a spell. Overhead, the wind creaks oak, and beneath me, thick grass bends. Tomorrow I will bring out the lawn mower, but today I catch a nap between them, the way I did when I was small, when their hands were warm and could touch me back.

I HAVE BEEN OLD all my life, my face like a piece of wood left out in snow and wind.

I was four when it happened. Papa had gone to get the grave diggers and bring them home to eat. He did that sometimes when it was hot and they were busy. Ma didn't mind cooking for a crowd.

But she had that day's meal fixed and waiting. She was already cutting apples for the next day's pie, and I was riding the broom in circles around the table.

"You getting too rowdy, Finch," Ma said. "Calm down."

"I'm playing circus," I told her. "I'm a pony rider."

"You've worn that pony out," she said. "Let him rest."

So I plopped down on the floor with the broom pony, ran my hand over the bristles, and pretended to rub his mane. Then I decided to get the pony some water. I needed a bowl. Ma had a bowl, but it was full of apples.

"I need a bowl to put some water in. My pony's thirsty."

"Give him some apple peels instead," Ma said. "He'll like that even better." She was good at playing along.

I was sitting beside the brown paper bag where Ma was dropping the peels. I reached in, grabbed a curled strand of red, and fed it to the pony. Then I looked up and saw the handle of a pot on the stove. "You still want some water?" I asked the pony, and when he said yes, I reached for the handle of that pot. I reached for the shine.

"LORD, LIZZIE," PAPA WHISPERED LATER, "ain't right for this child to be widowed by her own skin."

Ma shivered off oxygen soap, hard and brown, mixed it with honey and flour, and tried to paste my skin back on. She broke aloe fingers and doused my face, my shoulder and arm. She whispered, "I *told* her to stay away from that stove," her voice choking out. She brushed my hair away from the places where skin bubbled up.

They thought I was asleep, but I wasn't. I was dazed and drunk on honey water, lost in the buzzing of the burn. I thought they were washing my hair, but it was just blisters breaking and Ma crying, and water spilling from the cup they held to my mouth. I thought I might wash away.

They took me to the clinic for a day and a night, where my veins drank sugar water as nurses watched on.

At the time, it seemed like all my howls got lodged in my throat. I thought I was too stunned to make a sound. But Papa said I howled plenty, said I howled at the hospital and howled when I came back home.

Ma washed the shirt that Papa had cut away with his pocketknife. She kept it in the drawer, where it got buried by report cards and pictures. Discolored and tiny, it still smelled of grease when I threw it out. There's a stain in the bottom of the drawer where that shirt rested for thirty-odd years.

Not long after it happened, the grave diggers helped Papa screen in the porch because gnats kept landing on my body and drowning in my watery skin. Papa joked that he didn't want to claim ordinary bugs as family, and I had no choice but to sit outside. It was hot in the house, and I needed all the breeze I could get.

A man from the funeral home brought me a swing and hung it on the porch beam. He was a friend of Papa's, and Papa never forgot his kindness. Years later when his big heart broke open, Papa gave him the plot he'd been saving for himself. His daughter still brings flowers, and I straighten them after storms.

For a while following the scalding, people brought salves and remedies, sacred lards from beloved pigs. With baking soda and water, they made me masks and casts that stung the air out of my lungs. They baptized me in vinegars. They patted my thighs and said, "God bless."

For a while, parents slapped their children when they pointed. For a while, teachers punished the ones who called me "Granny Finch." But later, they all gave up. They all turned away. The ones without scars, they kept their secrets, hid their losses, lied in ways that only the living world does.

But you cannot hide the scars from a burn. Not with mud, the way I tried to when I was young, playing by the riverbank and smoothing clay into the dents on my shoulder and chest, filling it even until it dried white and broke. Sometimes I'd clay my face, splashing it wet to keep it smooth. In the water, I could almost see what I'd look like normal—my big dark hair curling wild and mushroomed around my head, my dark eyes, my face clay-smooth and drying white, then cracking into an old woman and washing off to leave me the same.

You can't hide burn scars, and there's no point in trying. I live in a world without secrets. That's why the children throw rocks. That's why the cordial adults smile and go back for one more stick of butter, one more box of Brillo pads when I enter the checkout line at the grocery. They never hold my gaze or stand too close.

I still live in the same house. At sundown, I lock the cemetery gate, honeysuckle and ivy growing around cast-iron posts. I cook myself supper, a piece of meat, something from the garden. I sit on the porch in the evenings, listening to the crickets, to the howling alley mutts. Sometimes the phone rings. Usually it doesn't. Sometimes I turn on the radio, but more often I hum. And when I'm tired, I sleep.

At sunup, I feed the animals, make coffee, read the paper. At seven, I open the gates. I speak with the funeral homes if there's a burial scheduled, nod to the workers coming in on bulldozers, and I'm civil with all the preachers who pass through. But mostly I trim hedges, straighten arrangements, pick up trash, and cut the grass. From time to time, I find new homes for spiders who've built webs in the armpits of crosses overlooking timid souls.

I tend this land. This land and the things that grow here are the only family I have left. With my scarred face and scarred neck and one scarred arm, I stake plots with wood and string, a room for you, a room for you. I bury the ones who died noisy in quiet, the ones who died lonely in family plots. The ones who died young, I cradle in boxwoods. Foes kiss here. Fears decompose. And in death, all the wounds begin to heal from the inside out.

So it don't matter when they call me "witch," and it don't matter when they turn away. Not too much, anyway. I have inherited what I remember. I am curator of this place.

IT'S A HOT day, mid-June, and I'm waiting for the sun to go down. I'm sweating from every pore and smelling ripe, smelling like sharp apples and mud, and waiting for an evening rain that probably won't come, and won't last long enough if it does.

I make my rounds at the cemetery, walking the perimeter, checking to make sure that all the cars are out, and I end up at the gate. Just in time.

"You gotta quit doing that, Finch," Leonard calls, kicking up dust as he walks toward me. He's pulled his blue squad car next to the cemetery gate, but I'm on the inside, locking up. I'm the one putting *him* behind bars.

"Doing what?" I ask him. "Have I done something to you?" Me and Leonard go way back. We went to school together, but we were never friends.

Leonard just shakes his head and takes a step closer. He's too fat for his policeman shirt, his belly leaning over his belt. His eyes are weak, blue, and afraid of mine. He scuffs his hard black shoes in the gravel, planting himself.

"I just talked to the preacher. He said Lois Armour had called him up crying. Said you'd paid her another visit."

"That ain't right, exactly," I explain. "I saw Lois on the street when I was walking to the mailbox."

"Well, okay. Then you saw her on the street. But, Finch, you gonna have to quit scaring people. You know as good as I do that her dead girl ain't sending messages from the grave. How come you want to addle that woman's head? Don't you reckon she's got troubles enough?"

"I got nothing to say to you," I tell him, and turn away, walking easy. The air feels damp, and I think we might get that shower after all.

"People's saying you crazy," Leonard hollers out.

"Can you arrest me for that?"

"Leave her alone, Finch," he says, and shakes the gate to let me know he's serious. And *mean*. He tries so hard to be mean.

But Leonard's guts quiver whenever I'm around. Everybody knows it. He's been scared of me since the day he walked into first grade and found the desk assigned to him, the one with "Leonard Livingston" written in block letters on red construction paper and taped to the wood. He was short for his age even then, and already shaped more like an egg than a boy. He placed his theme book in the space beneath his chair, his pencil in the groove cut into the wood, and then he turned my way.

I have a picture of the way I looked that morning. Ma had cut my curly hair short, parted it in the middle, and pulled it back with clips to either side. I had on a new blue dress with smocking at the top, and I was smiling—at least in the picture. But one whole cheek and jaw dripped into my neck, which dripped into my collar, and dribbled down my arm. It must have looked that way to Leonard the first time he saw me.

For when Leonard saw me, he startled, and his face

dissolved, too—into a slow pout—and then he jumped back and was crying and running toward the wall.

I just stared at him. I knew who he was already. He was the mayor's oldest son. Every Christmas, we got a card with a picture of his family on the front. Ma had shown me the card that morning before I left for school so I'd recognize somebody.

"His name's Leonard junior," she'd said. "I can't remember the baby's name, but he's a boy, too."

The teacher didn't move him on the first day, and Leonard cried until his eyes swoll shut. But on the second day, his mother came into the room, and then Leonard got a new seat, next to the windows, with the students whose last names began with A's and B's. I also recognized his mother, except in the picture, like Leonard, she smiled.

It was years before I looked back into Leonard Livingston's face. By then, I hated him.

He told me when we were nearly grown how sorry he was about that first day of school. I should've had pity on him. He was an outcast, too—fat, short, whiny—everything the mayor wouldn't want in a son. He was already destined to disappoint, almost as rejected as me. You'd think I could have sympathized. But I didn't.

And I don't sympathize with him much now, cranking up his old police car. He needs a new line. He comes by saying the same thing almost every day.

IT WAS BACK four years ago when we first got word of Lucy's death. The whole community grieved when they heard how she'd been shot, how her body was being flown home for burial.

"Why, I remember that little girl," Papa said. He was still alive then, but withered with arthritis and age. He sat in his special electric chair and fiddled with the buttons, moving up and down as he reminisced. "Lord, she was pretty, with that curly blond hair. *You* remember her, Finch. She won ever beauty pageant around when she was small."

"I don't think I know who she was," I answered, rubbing his twisted feet with Penetrol.

"Oh, sure you do. Remember the time the Vice President came to town—after the tornadoes came through? She was the little girl who sang the national anthem. Stood right up on the overturned trunk of that big oak in front of the library and sung like a lark. I'm sorry she met such a miserable end."

National anthem. National anthem. I couldn't remember ever hearing a little girl sing it.

"You say she's been murdered?" Miss Ashley Dugan asked me. She was visiting her husband's grave on the same day Lucy's was being dug. "I taught that child back fifteen, twenty years ago. I believe I had her for third grade. That just breaks my heart— she had such promise. And oh, she was funny, too. She wore tap shoes all the time. She danced *every-where* she went."

I tried to remember the shoes. It seemed like I should remember the shoes.

"Oh mercy." The funeral director sighed. "It's a sad day when you close the eyes of somebody as sweet-natured as that girl for the last time. Why, I remember when her mother came around asking for sponsorships to send her to a dance competition.

She could clog like nobody's business, but her family didn't have much money to spare. She came home with a trophy from that contest, too, and she brought it to us to keep in our family lounge. Bless her soul."

"You've seen her picture, Finch," one of the grave diggers insisted. "When she first ran away from home, they stapled flyers to all the light poles and ran her senior picture in the paper for a week. You had to see it. Everybody thought she'd been kidnapped."

"Shoot," another one said. "I can't believe she's gone," and he wiped a tear from his red cheek. "I went to *church* to sit next to that girl. I got saved six times just so she'd hug me. She was so pretty, the flowers bowed their heads when she went by."

But I didn't know her, and what I heard about her, I didn't like. I couldn't remember her at all. I recognized her house over on Glass Street. I reckon I must have seen her the way I see the other children, playing handball in the streets, or roller-skating down the sidewalk, and later, when they're teenagers, pushing around baby carriages or, maybe if they're smart, toting armfuls of library books. I must have seen her when she was small. She grew up a few streets away. But she was younger than me, a baby when I was in my teens. And she was unscorched. If I ever knew her, I paid her the same attention I pay all these other brats who scream and fight and light their cherry bombs in the streets. Which is to say none.

I have never invested much in beauty or trusted in sweetness. By the time she actually arrived, I was fairly unhappy about sharing my cemetery *with* her. It seemed for a while like people just loved her too much.

According to her marker, she was born on Christmas day

in '69. According to her marker, her name was Lucille Armour. Lucille Armour the beauty queen.

I had her pictured all wrong.

"I never liked that name," she told me the first time we talked. "I hated the way it clanked off my tongue. All those sharp angles—"

"But *Lucy Armageddon?*" I asked.

"Yeah," she said whimsically. "Lucy Armageddon. Now that's a name I can wear."

She told me that she'd changed her name legally five years before she died, but her family didn't like it. "I wanted to be somebody *else,*" she said. "I wanted to be somebody less lovely, more authentic."

I didn't have the heart to tell her that her family hadn't told the engravers about her new, authentic name.

Her stone is small and new—just two years old—because a temporary marker kept her plot for the first couple of years after she came here. I have it in my garden, the small copper plaque with her name, buried in jonquils. Lucy only got a permanent stone after the adult men's Sunday school class took up collections. Her mother won't work for fear of seizures and her father is bad to drink.

"Can you believe that?" she asked me when we'd known each other for a few weeks. "I don't even get a stone. My parents have no shame."

"They got no *money,*" I told her.

"They find money for things that are important," she replied. "Do you remember when I won the state baton-twirling championship?"

I shook my head no.

"You don't?"

"No."

And she laughed. "Well, anyway, Mama found money to send me to baton classes every day for the month beforehand. Because she wanted me to *win*. And you've seen all the pictures of me in all my dance costumes, haven't you?"

"No," I told her.

"Oh really? They're up in the auditorium. I guess they're still up. Well, anyway, she found money for the pictures because she thought she was going to get a modeling agency to take me on."

"I guess they just can't find money for a tombstone," I told her. "They're awful expensive."

But I didn't give a rip about her baton twirling or her tap dancing or her pictures either one. I liked the part of her that left all that. The part of her that changed her name and sliced her beautiful body so it would be more than just beautiful.

What binds us is the scars. Mine from burns, hers from a knife, and both of us numbed by them.

The day after her burial, I was picking the dead flowers out of her funeral spray while the Mediator was welcoming Lucille Armour. I wanted to get a peek at the beauty queen, anyway, the girl who everybody loved.

So I worked right above them, plucking through greenery while the Mediator and Lucy sat Indian-style, facing each other on the silky cushions of her coffin.

"She's not dead, is she?" Lucy asked the Mediator, and pointed right at me. "That's why she looks so thick?"

"Yes," the Mediator told her, and she was about to explain the way I move in and out of their world when Lucy announced, "She looks like she was skinned alive. What happened to her face?"

"Burned," I answered, and smiled at her and went back to my work, cleaning out the carnations. Lucy slumped back for a second, cowering in her bed. She looked to the Mediator, who was cutting her eyes up at me.

"Finch," the Mediator scolded. "I've told you over and over not to speak until I've explained the exceptions to the new folks."

"Sorry," I replied.

Then Lucy said, "Whew. Impressive scarring. Stop by later and I'll show you mine."

"Okay," I said, wondering what kind of scars beauty queens get. Little blisters from high heels on the backs of ankles?

And I moved on to trim a boxwood, since I had my clippers out.

I couldn't stop thinking about the new girl. She didn't look much like a beauty queen, and I couldn't figure out why. Usually the Mediator coaxes the body back to its predeath state when she first arrives at the coffin, before she opens it or wakes the person up. It scares a body to wake with holes in the head, with Y incisions stitched haphazardly along the torso after an autopsy. And while the hole in Lucille Armour's head had been filled in, her hair looked like a rat's nest. I wondered if there was a problem.

Later that day, I returned to Lucy's grave, and I've visited her every day since. She's my first real friend. She doesn't have a beautiful spot, but I've planted a weeping willow. It's skinny and slumps, but it's finally growing. I think that in time it may thrive. I sit beneath the new tree and tell her how it will shade her in summer, blanket her in winter, how the leaves will be a canopy for her one day soon.

"But yesterday, some boys climbed under the fence and broke off the tree I planted behind Hallie McBride. That tree cost me thirty dollars. I ought to find the little fools who broke it and beat 'em with it till the leaves fall off."

"Remember your blood pressure," Lucy jokes, then adds more seriously, "You shouldn't hate these children."

"They hate *me*. They try to tear up *every*thing I got."

"You'll be sorry," she says. "When you see the bigger picture, you'll feel bad."

"You hated me, too," I say, defending myself. "Don't get self-righteous on me."

"Sorry," she mutters.

And I get a little sad, and I tell her a thing I don't much say aloud. "These children—they're so afraid."

Then she tells me a memory: seven years old, in her bathing suit and tap shoes, curly-headed and lean. She had a cardboard box, and inside it, a kitten she couldn't keep. "Done got two dogs," her daddy had said. "Find it another home."

So Lucy was carrying it down the street, asking everybody she saw if they wanted a kitten. When it grew late and nobody had taken the kitten home, she began calling like a circus vendor, "Free kitten, free kitten." And apparently I heard her, though I don't remember. Lucy says we met near the firehouse, but I have no recollection. She tells me that I asked to see the free kitten, and that I asked her questions about where it came from (the woodpile) and why she couldn't keep it (her daddy said so). She tells me I asked her name and she told me, and that all the time I was asking questions, she was staring at my shoes.

That's what she remembers. My shoes! Red canvas sneakers fading to pink and folded-over blue kneesocks, she says.

"You remember my feet more than my face?" I ask her.

"No," she admits, sheepish. "But, Finch, you can't blame a

child for that. You gotta remember—you *look* different. Naturally, a child will react. But when you yell, you show them that they're right to fear you, so they go on fearing and hating people different from them. Now is that what you want?"

That Lucy. Those words. She's not always the voice of wisdom, but sometimes she says things just right. And I wish I'd known her sooner, when I could have kissed her face and she could have wiped mine dry.

I don't recall the shoes or socks, the cat I took home, or the child Lucille. I've worn so many pairs of shoes and fed a thousand strays. But I wish I'd remembered Lucy. Lucy, who dreamed for nights after of my melted face, of kittens that scratched and clawed. Lucy, who hitchhiked to Richmond on graduation night and took a bus to D.C.; who ran from the pageant life and her mama's instructions, "Just smile!"; who ran from her daddy to men so much worse; who came home in a zippered bag. I wish I'd remembered *her*.

Technically, I could be her mother—my body could have done it as surely as Lois Armour's did. But I'm not her mother, and Lucy was already old when she died. Old like me. Marked like me. Skin raised keloid, the slight purple of slugs. We have so much in common that sharing my voice with her is a natural instinct. I have taken her in.

And I don't torment her mother. I whisper one word. *Suicide.* I whisper it on the street, in the grocery line, at the polls on voting days. Whenever I see her, I say it beneath my breath. *Suicide.* I say it for Lucy.

Something is driving Lois Armour crazy, all right. But that something isn't me.

I KNOW THE WAY mothers go crazy. I lost Ma that way, my sweet ma, who let herself die over sins she didn't commit. In the days before my burning, while Papa was tending graves, Ma played with me all the time. We played library, and I got to be the librarian, and Ma was the little girl. We played Singing Sisters, and Ma cut cattails from the ditch, and we put on concerts for the squirrels. She let me help her in the garden. She let me play in the rain. She let me toss my dolls into mud holes, stir them around, and make doll soup.

She showed me trees to climb and taught me how to climb them. She knew the places to pick grapes and helped me fill my bucket. She took me to the circus and bought me candy cotton. And then one day when she wasn't looking, she let me burn off my face.

Ma never recovered from that. She kept herself alive for ten years after, but every day was a task. And she cried. My happy ma cried. She touched my cheek and wept like widows and orphans. Even years later, when I was healed, she cried that way.

Ma got skinny and distant. She didn't sit on the porch with me and Papa, and she didn't talk. She did the laundry and made the beds, kept the garden and cooked the meals, and she never complained. She never left the house anymore, and when Papa would send me on errands, she'd say, "Sam, you can't send *her*." She told me once that I didn't have to go to school if the children made fun of me. She told me she'd teach me herself.

And once when I came home hurt by words, insisting that I'd never show my face in public again, Ma pulled out her wedding dress, the dress she'd been saving for me, and she ripped the yellowed tulle and satin, pulling the skirt from the bodice to stitch me veils.

I swore I'd never wear them.

In the nights, she'd come to my bed and touch my scars, stroking my skin and crying sometimes. In the end, she couldn't even cry anymore, and her own fingers were nothing but dust on my cheeks. She died slow, eaten away by her own insides.

Ma loved me, but she didn't burn me. And the burns were hard to live with, but not as hard as being left stranded. Sometimes I get so mad, I kick her stone.

THERE IS WORK required of all who pass away. The Dead control the seasons. Everything depends on them. In June, the Dead tunnel earthworms, crack the shells of bird eggs, poke the croaks from frogs. The ones who died children make play of their work, blowing bugs from weed to weed, aerating fields with their cartwheels. They thump the bees and send them out to pollinate gardenias.

The ones who died old cue the roosters to crow and dismiss the dawn each morning. They time the tides, give directions to wind. They serve as midwives at animal births and reach out to stroke the dying sun's head until the rays spread pink and orange across the sky.

The ones who died strong push the rivers downstream, pull at clouds, and keep the sky in motion. They green the grass and tug it taller, grab tree trunks and stretch them upward in tiny bits.

The ones who died passionate kiss each bud and pinch its base until it pops open, surprised. The ones who died shy string spiderwebs, almost invisible. There's a job for everybody, on any given day. The Dead are generous with their gifts to the living.

Unless, of course, they are angry, and then they call the bees away so that nothing will bloom. When they are angry, the Dead catch the rain in their hands, bury it in their pockets, and laugh when the hard ground cracks.

But for now, it is June. The season is easy. The season is new. The Dead are content today.

The Dead always have their bodies to fall back on, but if they want to move through walls, they can take the shapes of termites. They can ride a breeze the way a song does. And, contrary to myth, they do not wear their burial garments for all eternity. Who would want to spend eternity in a musty Sunday suit? The Dead, they have some choices. They can wear whatever they like.

Lucy Armageddon wears tight patched jeans, a suede vest. Her hair stays knotted in light brown dreads—the way she grew it when she rejected pageantry and hot rollers—her face and arms still sunburnt. I watch her summoning clouds from her tombstone. She pauses to wave, and I'm glad her arms are strong. I'm needing a storm.

I work my way through the cemetery with my Weed eater, speaking to everyone I know. I meet Papa near the riverbank, Papa, who has only been dead for a couple of years. He still carries his smell, sweet and musky, like the deodorant he always wore. The traces of aftershave are fading, but Papa is still distinct to me. If he didn't turn to air when we hugged, I'd believe he was full-bodied.

"Where you off to?" I ask him.

"Gotta peel the skins from snakes today," he says. "Dangerous work, but somebody's gotta do it." And we laugh because the snakes won't see him at all. They won't even know he's been around.

"Where's Ma?" I ask. I haven't seen her much lately.

"Doing light duty," he says with a smile. "She's off to pinken tomatoes in all the gardens. She's getting so light that nobody much notices her anymore."

Ma has been buried almost thirty years. She's come a long way in that time. We will all be proud for her when she fades.

Papa asks if I need anything.

A mess of butter beans for supper, I tell him, if he sees somebody with nothing to do. I try to kiss him good-bye, but as usual, it's just a gesture, and he is gone.

When I go to be with the Dead, I feel it like a hazing, like the air before a summer storm, almost like a fog. The world around me opens, loosely woven, spaced for wind to sift through and blow my meanness out. But I never get there completely. I never get there in body. It's a partial reunion, with no way to really touch them except in my mind.

THE VEGETABLE MAN is still alive but smokes so hard and coughs so dark that he may not be for long. He comes each week, his rusty truck rattling predictably into the parking lot of the church just two blocks from the gate. Then he blows his horn three times long, two times short, and I can hear it all the way over here, even if I'm at the back of the cemetery, clipping the vines that grow along the fence. When the horn blows, I know that within the hour, the Vegetable Man will be stopping by.

He visits regularly in summer and fall, though I don't see him as much come winter. He has a cousin buried here, but most of his people are up in Petersburg.

I don't buy from him. He buys from me, at a discount. Sometimes I trade him squash for peas, potatoes for rutabagas or other things I don't grow.

"Damn almighty," the Vegetable Man says. "Not an ounce of fertilizer, you say?"

"Not an ounce."

My squash plants grow eight feet tall, sometimes ten. The potatoes come thirty to a hill some years. Though the Vegetable Man has seen my garden before, he shakes his head and laughs as he loads up his truck. He is old, with white stubble that never grows to a beard. He's worn the same boil on the side of his nose for as long as I've known him.

"God have mercy," he says. "My wife could make drawers out of them squash leaves, and she's got an *ass* on her, too." He laughs and coughs, and bits of the raw turnip he's been chewing spray into the basket of onions.

The back of his truck is full of rust and dirt. He's built a wooden awning over the truck bed, but now the wood is dark and softened, shadowing the vegetables but not offering much protection from rain. The brown paper sacks are held down by a bushel of string beans, a half-bushel of okra. Today he pays me in quarters and crumpled bills, pulling money from every pocket and a greasy five from beneath his hat. He throws in a couple of pears, "to have with your supper," he says.

At the store, they've stopped selling my vegetables—since Reba Baker took over and made the place a "Christian establishment." They say it's unnatural for cucumbers to grow so fast, so long. I ask them what they think fertilizer *is*. And ain't nothing never died in their yard? A possum or coon? I've been eating my vegetables all my life and couldn't die if I tried. I tell them that, but the only time they sell what I've grown is when the Vegetable Man does it for me, without their knowing.

"You going to the store?" I ask him.

"Done been," he says. "Reba made me swear I hadn't been up here 'fore she bought anything. Sniffed everything I sold her to see if it stunk of death."

"She thinks death stinks, she ought to get a whiff of her breath," I retort.

Then the Vegetable Man cackles and shakes his head. "You being nasty, Finch. Reba ain't that bad."

"Maybe what's bad to you's different from what's bad to me," I say. "But I got no use for Reba Baker. She *claims* to be Christian, *claims* to do good and love everybody. But don't matter how many raffle tickets she sells to help crippled children. Don't matter. She's full of hate and venom."

"You women fight ugly," he says as he climbs into the cab of his truck. "I ain't getting involved. No siree, I'm just gone take these pickins I got from you and sell 'em over at Foxbridge. You ain't gotta worry. I can *sell* your vegetables." He cranks up, and his engine rattles like loose dentures. "See you directly."

When he's gone, I wash off the pears at the outside spigot for fear he's spit turnips on them, too. I put one in my pocket and bite into the second. It's sweet, but not as sweet as the ones on the tree next to Ma's grave.

A cat I don't recognize rubs between my ankles, and I pick it up and scratch its ears. It purrs and tries to climb into my mouth, smelling the pear that somebody else grew. Sweet cat. I drop it on the ground and jingle the change in my pocket. Two dollars in silver, three dollars in ones, and an oily five. Money I don't particularly need. It's not about money, selling the vegetables. I'd give them away for free. It's not about money at all.

I try to imagine the hands that picked these pears. I try to imagine the hands that planted the pear tree that grew the pear I'm eating. I try to imagine the yard that tree is in. Or is it a grove? A graveyard? I try to imagine the Dead who called down the storm that watered that tree that grew the pear that I eat.

I decide that tomorrow I'll see Reba myself. I'll pay her in change and wait while she counts it. If she won't eat my vegetables, I'll make her take my money. In one way or another, she'll handle what I've touched.

THE NEWEST GRAVE here belongs to William Parker Blott. Unlike most people who are buried first and later crowned with a headstone, Blott and his monument arrived together, a week after he died. His family paid the engravers so much money that they stopped what they were doing to design Blott's new home. And what a home it is! It took two ton trucks and a crane just to place it. We'd never seen anything like it before.

William Blott woke to death disillusioned. Like everyone else, he was disappointed to find that death wasn't what he'd thought. There were no lounge singers singing his name, no chorus lines kicking to welcome him here. There were no photographers snapping pictures, no symphonies, no hullabaloo. There weren't even the predictable things—the saints waiting by walls of jasper, the harp music. There was no deep-flowing river with a raft waiting to carry him across. He was not reborn into a different body. Not a child, a tree, or a common bug. He was not unconscious, as he'd hoped.

And he was most definitely not at rest.

In the grave beside him, a baby was weeping shrill.

The Mediator welcomed him and shook his slippery hand. "William Parker Blott," she said. "Welcome, William Parker Blott." The Mediator, with her periwinkle robe, the gold pipes shining in her hair, she told him the facts. "You sleep in the coffin, you work in the air. Think of it as a pantry. In life, you lived on just one shelf. Now you're on two. The one above life, the one below, to help you see where you've been. To teach you how to be honest."

The others waited to see how he'd respond, shaking their heads, tittering.

"You're heavy now," the Mediator told him. "You won't rise up for a while. Our whole business here is to lighten, and when you're wholly weightless, you'll move to the next level."

Sheri Reynolds

"Ugh," Blott said.

"I know," the Mediator told him. "Those morticians overdo it with the glue," and she moistened his lips with vinegar to break the seal.

The curious neighbors watched him recover his muscles and test his fingers and toes. The ones from plots far away tiptoed closer, peeking to see his face.

"It works like this," the Mediator explained. "The Dead coax the natural world along. We're responsible for weather and tides and seasons. For rebirth and retribution. You're going to enjoy it, I'm sure. But if you want to know *real* enlightenment, you've got to lose the weight. All of it. And we're not just talking about blubber here, either. We're talking about burdens and secrets, buster. This is critical information, so listen up.

"In this place you've moved beyond experience. Now it's your stories that keep you down. You can't leave until you've told them."

William Blott, never much of a talker, moaned, and the Mediator touched his head. The way he recoiled, she might have been a serpent or an apparition, a dangerous thing indeed.

"You don't have to worry," she comforted. "You won't be lonely. You'll learn a great deal about yourself and your kind. There *are* advantages."

"Not too many advantages," I whispered to Lucy. "He's got the plot next to *Marcus Livingston!*"

"He's in for a surprise," Lucy said. "I hope he likes babies with big lungs."

And sure enough, it wasn't long until Marcus began to squall full volume. William Blott collapsed into a ball and hid his ears.

The next evening, I was trimming the grass around the

edges of Papa's stone, my hands and knees denting the earth. "He's never gonna speak at this rate," I told Papa.

"You might be right," he answered. "Then there'll be two of 'em up on that hill sitting heavy and turning the ground to acid. I don't know how Rulene Thornton stands it, making her home up there."

"I think he'll be okay," Ma breathed. "He'll talk when he's good and ready. He spent most of his life by himself. You can't expect the man to become a talker just because he's come to a place with so many ears."

"I know," I said. "But I'm awfully curious."

Papa winked at me and laughed. "It ain't like you don't know nothing about him, Finch. The man was nearly 'bout a local celebrity before he died."

"Yeah, but he's such a mystery."

"Everyone's a mystery until they tell their own story," Ma said.

In those first days, when the dirt was still red and showing around William Blott's burial space, I scattered grass seed over the ground, and Lucy called a cloud to water it for me. We were nosy, spying to find out whatever we could.

He kept his back to us the whole time, but he was sitting up by then, inside his special tomb, slumped over, clearly depressed.

"You know, we're not that bad," Lucy called. "You might like us if you gave us a chance."

"How long's he been crying? That baby?" William Blott asked her, surprising us both. I ducked behind Rulene Thornton's cross, in case he turned around, but he didn't.

"No one's exactly sure," Lucy told him. "Miss Lizzie Nobles says he was crying when she got here, and that's been almost thirty years."

"What's the matter with him?"

"Who knows?" she answered. "He's never said anything. I don't know if he couldn't ever talk or if he just forgot how. The crying gets worse every day."

"That's too bad," William Blott said.

Day by day, he got more and more curious, peeking from his tomb when everyone had gone about their doings, calling out to Marcus and studying other nearby stones.

He never dodged me, though. He didn't think I could see him. He didn't even run to hide when I was near. For all practical purposes, I was invisible to him, just a regular groundskeeper with my heart pumping fine.

"I think he's coming around," I told Ma as I scrubbed dark mildew from her stone. "He's like a scared cat hiding beneath the bathtub. He keeps sneaking out in secret."

"Pretty soon, when the place is familiar, he'll come out regular," she said. "You just wait."

And sure enough, William Blott began talking. But like everybody else, he crouched behind voices at first, trying to maintain his image.

When the Mediator asked him one night how things were going, he hid behind his grouchy voice: "They'd be a hell of a lot better," he said, "if somebody would shut that baby up!"

But the image corroded, as images will. William wasn't a natural grouch, so he couldn't keep it going.

When he tried to be a comedian, it was the intonation that failed him, his jokes about as funny as a tidal wave. When he tried to talk like a British scholar, he got dirt in his mouth and wound up coughing, done in by the accent that time.

When he tried to pretend that he was comfortable with

death, that there was nothing in his past he needed to release, he began to stutter.

I pieced together his story in bits, given in all different voices. I compared his story with what I knew of him already and added it up for myself.

William Parker Blott lived poor and died rich. Around the neighborhood, everyone considered him a bum—we didn't think he had a pot to piss in. We didn't know he had family or money, either one—until he was on his deathbed. Then suddenly he was found, long-lost father, son of wealthy blue bloods. His only child, Rhett, came just once and, shamed by the destitution his father had chosen, he paid off the doctor bills and funeral home. He paid for a high-class coffin and a one-man mausoleum, with BLOTT in large letters over an arched doorway. Inside, William Blott rests in white marble, like a king, a stained-glass picture of Jesus hanging above him. His family didn't want him buried like common country people. Even if he'd had an alcohol problem, even if he'd abandoned his young wife and son, he would not be buried like a pauper.

Then the son offered to pay Reba Baker and the adult women's Sunday school class who had taken on William as a Good Samaritan project. When the women told him there was no need, he made them this offer: Anything that his father owned was theirs. They could raffle it off, use it themselves, donate it to Goodwill, or have a flea market. They deserved compensation, Rhett Blott said. For he was a businessman, taking care of business. It was all just business to him.

Didn't he want some sort of memento? Reba asked him. Would he like for some of the deacons to accompany him to the place his father had lived?

But Rhett said no.

So the land that William Blott had lived on, that tangled, overgrown property where no one had ever been invited to visit, could belong to the Sunday school class, too. Rhett Blott declared that his word was gold and he left before supper on the second day after William had died. He didn't want to spend another night in a second-rate motel with only rooms, no suites. He'd have his lawyers draw up the papers. The inheritance would be theirs in a matter of weeks.

Reba Baker couldn't believe it. They'd use his house for a boys' and girls' club. They'd sponsor vacation Bible schools or maybe even Christian camps for children as far away as the coast. Somebody'd have to build a road in and out, but surely T & T Construction would donate a bulldozer for the church's use.

"What they don't know yet," William tells us, "is that I never built a house. There's not even a water pump on that property." Then he laughs, but his laugh is a sad one and goes on too long. I can feel the ground tremble just a bit, no more than the way it trembles when the teenagers play their music too loud.

"Poor old Reba," he says. "She's a good old gal."

William has begun to catch on. The ones who've just died tell the stories. They do the talking, repeating the things they remember.

The others comment sometimes. Not always. It isn't always important.

And the wisest voices speak least. As in life, the wise ones have usually been around the longest. They've had the most time to harvest insight. They speak softly as they lighten, fade away.

The newest of the Dead have to lean into their own deaths

to hear them. The wisest of the Dead are pushed away, bit by bit, by the understanding of the new.

But there's more to it. The stories make it bearable to be. The stories make it bearable to have lived at all.

So William tells his story to warm them. He tells it to keep the coolness of nights out of the hollows and cracks in their bones. New voices are warmer than old ones, and stories that haven't been told are wool compared with the cotton of things already said. Still, I have to strain to hear, as night grows deeper, and I am forced by the darkness away.

I put my ear to the ground over Lucy's grave and listen with her. I put my fingers in the grass and pretend it's her hair, that I can stroke it. I lie with her there, breathing earth and listening to William.

"I'm certainly not proud of what I did," William says. "I shouldn't have married or had that boy, but I was young. I didn't know any better. I'd just returned from Korea, and I was doing what I thought I should. I couldn't keep a job, and Daddy kept having to buy things for Rhett and Pearl—that was my wife. He bought Pearl a car. Of course, he'd already given us the house. I shouldn't have run off and left them, but I knew they'd have a better life without me. I knew Daddy'd take care of them better than I could."

"Responsibility," some old fart shouts. "Responsibility is a virtue seldom learned." He adjusts his hearing aid and settles back down in his coffin, where he sleeps.

Then Marcus Livingston begins to cry. William tries to talk over him at first, but voices yell, "Huh?" and "What?" The voices rake over and the baby screams and William's voice is left behind, until he gives up.

Then he begins humming, and the voices cease. He hums the way wind blows through wheat, and the baby falls asleep.

"My God," Lucy says. "Can you believe that?"

"That fellow's *all right!*" Papa cheers.

"Bless his bones," Ma mutters.

"Glory hallelujah," the Poet sings.

All around the cemetery, the Dead sit up, cheering for William Blott, giving each other high fives and winks.

"Would you let the man speak!" the Mediator insists, but she's laughing, too, because nobody's ever been able to soothe Marcus. Not even the Mediator herself.

"For the first ten years, I lived off the land," he continues. "Squatting in hunting cabins when I could. I slept in a warehouse for a long time. And I don't remember where all I stayed. I camped in rest areas and airport lobbies until guards threw me out. I slept in little children's tree houses sometimes."

"You're telling us where you *slept*," the Mediator states. "Tell us about your*self.* Tell us the most amazing thing you ever saw."

"Well," William continues. "Hmmmm."

Around the graveyard, we all wait to hear.

"This doesn't seem too important, but I guess the most amazing thing I ever saw was a cat with the head of a squirrel in its mouth. It doesn't seem too important, though." He looks around distrustful, like he's expecting to be the butt of a joke.

"Keep going," the Mediator tells him, and everybody nods.

"Well," William says, "the cat was dragging that squirrel through the woods, with the whole body drooping between its two front feet. And the squirrel was still alive. I could see it kicking."

"*That's* something," the Mediator says. "Why do you think you remembered that particular image?"

"I don't know." Blott hesitates. "I suppose the cat carried the squirrel off somewhere and killed it. But I always imagined the inside of that cat's mouth, how the squirrel must have gnawed at his tongue. I don't know. For all I know, the squirrel got away."

Then, almost like an apology, he says, "I don't remember a lot of things. I used a lot of drugs. It's not something I'm proud of."

"Them drugs'll get you every time," Ma whispers, and a former construction worker from the north side agrees.

"Yeah," William continues, returning quickly to the comfort of his life summary. "But finally, after a good many years— maybe fifteen years on the streets—I'm in a shelter and the person serving soup is from Richmond, from the same neighborhood where I grew up. And he contacted Daddy, and next thing I know, Daddy's at the shelter. I don't think anybody from around here knew my daddy. He did most of his dealings up the road a hundred miles or more. He was a tough man, and when he came to the shelter, it wasn't a family reunion or anything of the sort. He didn't want me to shame him, and he didn't really want me to come back home. But he brought me a picture of my boy, and he arranged for me to go to a rehab clinic.

"After thirty days, they let me out and handed me an envelope with a letter from Daddy. That's when he told me about his property here. You know how he described it? He called it 'Ten acres, uncleared, in a primitive little place where nobody knows you.' That's how I wound up here."

"Primitive little place, my ass," Papa says.

"I always liked it here," Blott whimsies. "People let me be for the most part. I had a good life until the cancer eat me up."

"You had cancer?" a voice calls. "I had cancer, too."

"Did you say you're from up near Richmond?" someone else asks. "That was my old stomping ground."

"I recognize you from the store," another one tells him.

And so it is that William Blott makes himself at home, slowly, finding himself connected to others in a thousand different ways.

In the open air, the night is humid, though it is always cold underground. I feel my own face slick, perspiration rolling off my sides. I lie over Lucy, sweating, wondering what would sprout if I could make my body water hers enough.

IN THE NIGHT, I dream of a cat in my mouth, its legs draping down and clawing at my face and chest. I wear the cat like a long, stubborn beard.

In my mouth, the cat clamps its teeth around a squirrel's neck, and the tiny paws and bushy tail of squirrel kick in my throat. I dream the squirrel gnaws the tongue of the cat, biting it off at the root.

Then I dream I am speaking before a room of burning people, my assignment: to teach them to put out fires. But when I open my mouth, I have someone else's tongue. It is too small and too rough, and all it will do is call me a fool for believing that flames can be extinguished with words.

I GET TO THE STORE EARLY. It's the first Saturday in July, and the weather's already so hot that the supper scrapings have spoiled in trash cans by breakfast. Even the dogs won't eat leftovers when it's this hot. And people know better than to leave that trash in the house overnight. Summers here smell like watermelon rinds gone soft, like the plastic wrapped around grocery-store chickens, like sour milk and cantaloupe, just-cut grass and salty slabs of bacon.

I order a biscuit and sit down on a stool next to the lunch counter. Reba makes small talk with the men gathered there before work. I don't know them, but they nod to me and try not to stare. One of them tells Reba that they're working a construction site, that they're not from around here.

She takes her time getting me my biscuit, but I've got all day. When I run out of coffee, I step right behind the bar and fill up my cup. She cuts her eyes, but I pay her no mind, and when the men have gone and she can't think of anything else to do, she goes ahead and serves me.

It's the worst biscuit I've ever eaten, but I don't mention that. I eat it like it's candy.

"See here," Reba says after a time. "I've told you before and

I mean it, Finch Nobles, I don't want none of them vegetables coming in here. You hear me?"

I don't say a word. I stare her right in the eyes until she darts her eyes away and starts wiping down the counter with one of them handy dish towels that you can use all day and then throw out. One of the construction workers had spilled a little salt, and Reba treats it like a nuclear disaster, careful to get every grain.

"I got nothing against you," she continues. "It ain't personal. But there ain't no telling what happens to a body after it's dead. No telling what sorts of gasses it gives off. And I ain't wanting to be the cause of nobody's sickness because they ate the prettiest tomato they ever seen, picked right out of your garden. You hear me? I'm running a *Christian* establishment."

I drain my cup and hold her gaze until she turns to the grill and begins cleaning it. She pours water on it, and white smoke poofs, then passes as she scrapes burned drippings away.

"See here, I ain't wanting no bad feelings with you, but you burying 'em too close to your house, Finch. That Larrimore boy that died in the car crash a few months back is just about in your yard. And poor old William Blott is at the top of the hill that runs right down to your garden. And he died of a *tumor*. One good rainstorm's all it'll take—"

"For God's sake, Reba," I tell her. "Don't you know what happens to a corpse? It gets sealed up so tight that a Genesis flood couldn't wash out the chemicals."

"You tell me what I'm smelling then, when it rains too hard in the summer and I walk by them drains. You tell me."

And I don't have an answer for her on that count. There *is* a certain sweetness I can't explain.

Then a police car pulls up, and it's Leonard, of course. He's the only officer that works this area. He's slow to get out, slow to make his way to the door. He's even slow pushing it open, so that the bell that tinkles to alert Reba of a customer rings longer and quieter than usual.

Reba increases her volume to make sure that he hears. "I smell that formaldehyde in the drains ever time it rains. And if it's in the drains, it's in the ground. And if it's in the ground, it's in your bell peppers, and I ain't selling 'em here." She punctuates her speech with a nod of her head in Leonard's direction. He's taken a seat at the lunch counter, but he's skipped a chair, so that there's an empty space between us.

"How much do I owe you?" I ask her, and then I begin counting it out in change as she gets Leonard's coffee. I use all the pennies first.

"For all I know, we could end up with cancer, with William Blott just barely dead, bless his soul, and them tumor cells trickling down to your tomato bushes."

"Now, Reba," Leonard says. "I think you're out of line."

"I might be, but I ain't selling them vegetables in *this* store. There's been dead buried on that hill for a hundred years."

"Sixty," I say.

"And the way disease spreads, and when nobody knows what it is that causes cancer, and with all the things killing people today, you got to be cautious," she adds. "I was doing my best to help out William Blott, and I approached him with Christian kindness. But he was a filthy man, covered in sores, and he's buried right on that hill with drug addicts and common trash, and as far as I know, he didn't even clean up his *soul* before he died, the Lord help him."

"My baby brother's buried next to Blott," Leonard defends. "And it don't bother me a bit. There's a lot of other good people up there, too. That graveyard's clean and kept up better than any I know. Finch does a fine job with that."

"Thank you, Leonard," I tell him. "But there's no point. Reba likes being ignorant."

And Reba keeps going on about how she intends to pray for me, but in truth, I'm more surprised to be defended by Leonard than to be chastised by Reba.

"I'm gone pray for your soul," she hollers. "You keep company with dark spirits and you'll never see the pearly gate."

"To hell with you," I tell her as I'm walking out. And Leonard drops his head to hide what might be a smile.

T HE DEAD MAY fertilize my garden. They may even darken the silks on my corn. But I haven't yet convinced them to do the picking. I take a foot tub and head for the land I tilled and planted myself. I might be slight, but my shoulders are broad from working like an ox all my days. I carry my own firewood and I move my own furniture. My arms are like cables, and my will is stronger still. I climb my own pecan tree each fall, tie thick ropes around the branches, and jump to the ground. I hook the ropes to the tractor and drive, shaking those limbs until the pecans fall like hail.

And then I pick them up, heaving brown paper bags. And yes, my back hurts the next morning. But lugging around the things I cultivate is not a burden to me. Even if I grow stiff with it, I love every minute, from the planting to the weeding to the watching to the harvesting. I love every plant like a daughter.

Gardening is something I've done all my life. Even as a child, I planted the seeds of apples and grapes. I sucked the pits of peaches down to the tiniest orange strings, and I planted the hard nuts that remained at the edge of the yard. Some of them sprouted and some didn't. I planted rotten persimmons and potato eyes, and I grew plants and harvested fruits in the most unlikely places.

Now in the warm season, I can feast out of my own yard. I can work in the dirt until dark. And tonight I have worked so late that I've forgotten to close the gate. Leonard's the one who reminds me.

"Aye, Finch?" he calls, and I startle.

I'm at the spigot, washing the dirt off the back side of a watermelon, except now, the watermelon is dirty again.

"You surprised me," I tell him. "What do you want?"

"Nothing. Just came by to be sure everything's okay. It's heading toward dark and the gate's still open. I noticed it driving by—"

I study him in the dim light. He shifts his weight and eyes the ground where a wormy kitten rolls at his feet. Another one comes up and rubs against his pants leg—wild little kittens that have never let me touch them, and Leonard scratching their ears.

Then he peeks back up at me and says, "That's a hell of a melon."

I rinse it off again, turning it beneath the water like a globe.

The deep green irregular bands cut into the paler green like mountain ranges traversing long distances.

"I got three or four more ripening," I tell him. "Didn't plant but a few hills of watermelon this year." And I offer the melon to him, holding it out, with water running back up my arms.

"I can't take it, Finch," he says. "But thank you just the same."

"Can't or won't?" I push. "You scared to eat what grows here?"

"Nah," he claims. "It's just that ain't nobody at the house but me, and it won't get eat."

"You can share it with your folks," I suggest.

He shakes his head. "We're on the outs. Father's disappointed I didn't get promoted." He looks down.

"Sounds like all the more reason for me to give you a melon," I tell him, and step forward with it, almost pushy. "You can take a few of them kittens with you, too, if you'll have 'em. Must be ten little wild ones running around."

When he takes the watermelon, he holds it the way a man holds a baby the first time—tentative and away from his body, its weight balanced between his two hands.

In the distance, I hear a baby's cry, high-pitched and whole-lunged.

I walk Leonard back to his police car.

"'Preciate it," he says, sitting the melon in the passenger seat.

But then the kittens are there, too, sniffing inside the police car, and when I reach to shoo them, they hiss. But when Leonard reaches down, they ram their heads against his big fingers.

"They had their shots?" he asks me.

"No," I tell him. "Do they look like they've had shots?

They're wild." But I feel stupid for saying it, because they're tame enough with him.

He lifts them both into the car, tossing them into the back-seat, where they bat at old coffee cups and trash.

Then he reaches out and shakes my hand. His hand is cold, but what I notice most are his hairy knuckles, how black and sporadic that hair.

In the distance, I hear a baby's cry, and I remind myself to lock the gate on time from this day on, before Leonard has a chance to come back in and upset the balance of things.

MOST BABIES FADE quick. Most babies are so light that they're pushed out right away—by the next few people who come along. Most babies don't have a story to hold them down.

But Marcus Livingston does. He just can't tell it.

In the nights, he cries, waking me wherever I'm sleeping. Sometimes curled up on the porch with the cats, I mistake his voice for an animal in heat. His screams are sharp with needing, like the female cats I keep.

If I'm in bed, I jerk deep into my quilt to layer myself from his crying. Sometimes his cries are the throaty *waaaas* of newborns, and sometimes the screams of toddlers. Sometimes his cries are the cries of a man the age he would have been if he'd lived—a man in his thirties and horribly hurt. His cries age and retreat. Maybe that's what makes them so horrible, those cries without words. There is no blanket or pillow thick enough to protect me from the noise.

Sometimes when I'm stretched above Lucy, damp with sweat and dew, I leap to my feet before I'm awake. And even when I'm standing, his crying vibrates the small bones of my feet.

No matter where I sleep, when Marcus cries, I awaken. I wish for only one thing: quiet. I would like to soothe him, but there's nothing for me to hold. And the Dead insist that he must be allowed to wail. "Until he finds his way," the Mediator says.

Sometimes when I'm especially tired or especially content, curled up in a soft place, in a soft way, when I'm dreaming easy and resting fine and his nighttime fits interrupt, I want to choke the screams right out of baby Marcus.

"I'd like to knock that child on up to Jesus," I say to Lucy.

"Maybe you need to help him instead," she replies, yawning. She's patient about most things, even in sleep. It's one of the things she's learned since dying.

"Help him *how*? You tell me how a baby can have a story to tell."

"You could teach him to talk, I guess. And ask him."

I try to sleep, but my mind gets tangled, figuring what kind of story Marcus could hold. He was born privileged. He got plenty to eat. I never visited his house, but I know he must have had a store-bought crib softened by white blankets with rabbits and cottages and trees delicately embroidered.

His ma was the *mayor's wife*, who wore pillbox hats and pressed-hem skirts. The mayor's wife, who cut the ribbon when the library opened, who traveled all the way to New York City to see a show and wrote a story about it for the local paper. The mayor's wife, who lunched with the wife of the governor and who drove a Cadillac, who sent off the black-and-white pictures of her boys and got back portraits in oil that still hang in the library. Baby Marcus had it good with those fine folks.

But Leonard, the oldest son, was a lumpy, cross-eyed boy. "There must have been some mistake at the hospital," Papa used to joke. "With parents like his, and that boy so brooding. He pure-tee looks inbred."

"Sam," Ma would say, "you better hush talking like that."

But it was true. Leonard, the first son, was scared of dogs and ran between his daddy's knees whenever they got too close. The mayor pushed him out and made him pet the dogs, even if he cried.

"You act like a girl," the mayor would say, ashamed.

Leonard, the first son, wore glasses with square black frames. He stood shorter than the other boys, even though his father was tall. Thick-tongued and snaggletoothed, he could not say his s's, and the children teased him almost as much as they teased me. I was glad for every time he stumbled, for the day he peed himself in class, for every time he went to the board and subtracted his equations wrong. Though Leonard sucked the attention away, I probably hated him more than anybody else, and when other kids taunted, "You so ugly that when you were born, your daddy puked and your mama passed out," I laughed harder than anyone.

It was even funny after the children turned to me and said, "What you laughing at, Granny?" or "Shut up, Witchy-Bird."

On the day the new courthouse was dedicated, the year I was in first grade, the mayor's family stood on the courthouse steps without Leonard, with just the baby, Marcus, in his mother's arms.

"Wonder where their older son is?" Ma asked, but I just shrugged.

The mayor said a little speech, and while he was talking, I spotted Leonard off to the side and wondered why he was kept back with the nanny when the pictures were being made.

Baby Marcus laughed at the photographers. Though he wasn't quite a year old, he called out and laughed to the crowd, and the jovial mayor said, "That's my boy." When the baby started crying, the mayor joked that he had a politician's lungs.

The mother tried to hush him, and someone from the crowd said, "Poor little fellow. He needs a nap."

"He won't sleep," his mother explained, and some of the women nearby nodded knowingly about colicky babies.

That day was the last public appearance of Marcus Livingston, and as he left, the mayor held him up and said, "Wave, boy. Tell 'em bye."

The baby, who was done with his crying by then, waved to the crowds. But he waved backward.

I remember that scene because Papa said, "Looka there, Finch. He's waving good-bye to hisself," and Papa lifted me up on his shoulders so I could see, and I pretended, for a minute, that I was in the mayor's family—a rich little girl without scars from burns or holes in her socks, waving like that baby, held up by somebody important. I thought Leonard Livingston was a fool for missing such a grand opportunity.

Not many weeks after, I sat on the screened-in porch with Ma and watched the cars file into the graveyard like soldiers marching. The governor came to the funeral and rode in a car with a tiny flag flying from the hood. A tiny flag for a tiny baby in a tiny little grave. They drove around the house and behind the big hill, then up to the top, where they parked. And Marcus was buried way up there. From my swing, I could see the people gathered at his grave site, tiny moving dots. There were so many people that the cars spilled into our yard and outside the cemetery, on the streets.

From my swing, I could hear his mother weeping. It was winter, and the cold made my nose run and reddened my ears, but still I stayed on the porch, watching and listening, wondering how it could be that a baby as lucky as Marcus had died. His family had money enough to go to Richmond, where they had doctors who knew more about babies than adults.

Everyone suspected that the mayor wished it was Leonard who'd died. Probably even Leonard knew it, because after that, he got fat, like his body was trying to take up enough space for two boys—not just one. And after that, I felt sorry for Leonard for a little while and I didn't laugh so much when he was teased.

Nobody knew what had happened to Marcus. The family said he'd died in the night. On his death certificate, the doctor wrote "failure to thrive," and in my mind, I compared it to the tiny pines I'd found near the river and moved into the yard. I'd watered them, tended them, and they'd died anyway, like Marcus. I considered it "failure to thrive" when they dried up and the small needles broke away from the stick of their trunks. But I knew that I may have watered them too much, or stepped on them by accident once or twice.

It wasn't until years later that I thought of Marcus Livingston again. I was fifteen, without friends, with no figure to speak of, no talents or plans for my life, and with my ma just past buried. I had Papa to take care of, but he kept busy all the time to keep from thinking. He took up motors, tinkering with them late in the nights. He fixed the lawn mowers and tractors himself in the little shed behind the house. He put them together and took them apart, and greased all the pieces and went back to work.

I did my lessons after school and walked down to the river. I had a bike, and sometimes I rode it between tombstones. I planted my flowers and picked them for Ma's grave, and in the nights, I had dreams of vases and flowers in all sizes and shapes. In my dreams, I had to arrange them, and I arranged them over and over: daisies in blue glass and roses in clear, gladiolias in buckets, mums and phlox in old soup cans, again and again, like puzzles. Some nights as soon as I'd get an arrangement finished, it'd burst into flames. I'd have to put out the fire with the water from other vases. Then the flowers from vases without water withered, and so on.

I cooked sometimes, but mostly we ate sandwiches. We bought hams and turkeys, cut them to slabs, and ate them on white bread with mustard.

In the evenings, I'd sit in front of the mirror with slices of meat, plastering them damp to my face and imagining what I'd look like with skin unwithered. The meats we bought presliced were best, though the turkey was too white, the ham too pink. They did not make pressed beef—or at least they didn't sell it where I grew up, and it would have been too dark anyway. But in the evenings, in front of the mirror, I could smooth it to my face and neck and pretend.

I went through a stage where I slept that way, thinking that maybe the cure had never been discovered. Maybe burns could be cured with ham on the cheek, bonded with jellyish fat to my skin. I tricked myself into thinking that perhaps I'd wake up with skin thriving, and I began to wear the wedding-dress veils so that when I woke, I could pull back the veil and be surprised by the evenness of my face.

I was disappointed each morning. And if my soul could have divorced my body, it would have. Every day that I woke up burned and stinking of meat, I saw myself uglier, a remnant of a girl. I looked to the ground, uneven like my face, and took consolation in the textured earth. But after a while, I grew too ugly to go to school, to go to the store. After my ma was dead, there was nothing left to prove. I could go ahead and admit how ugly I was.

"You're pretty as a picture," Papa would say, and when I'd cry about my face, he didn't understand. "You been this way for a long time, Finch," he'd remind me. "It looks better than ever. Ain't you used to it yet?"

He didn't know what to do when his words made me quiet. So he grew quiet, too. Together we walked to Ma's grave, and he'd stop by trees, take my hand, say, "Feel," and rub my palm against the bark. "Your beauty's like a *pine's*," he'd say. It was all he could do. It was all he could muster. He found more comfort mowing the grass and trimming hedges than he found with me.

The boys from the high school drove by in their Fiats and Volkswagen Bugs, rolling down the windows and hollering out that so-and-so wanted to take me on a date.

Papa'd look up from his newspaper and ask, "Do you wanna go out with that boy, Finch?"

"They're making *fun* of me," I'd snap.

"Now, you don't know that," Papa'd say. "Maybe that boy wants to take you to a show."

But one night, some boys dared each other to break into

the cemetery, climb into my bedroom window, and kiss me good night. It was a rite of passage for some club they were forming, and we didn't have any haunted houses in the neighborhood. I was the next best thing.

But they clanked the ladder against the house and woke us up. Papa met them outside, just as I stuck my head out to see what was going on.

The boy on the ground ran away, yelling terrible things, but Papa caught the one who'd been climbing.

Papa had strong arms and shook the truth right out of him.

"Why *my* daughter?" Papa asked him.

"Just 'cause," the boy said.

"None of that," Papa scolded, the boy's hair waving as Papa jostled him. *"Why my daughter?"*

And I called to Papa, "Just let him go," because I was worried that the one who'd run would come back with friends. Because I didn't really want to hear the boy's answer.

"'Cause—you know—of the way she looks."

"And how does she look?" Papa asked him.

"She's . . ."

"How does she *look?*" Papa asked again. And the boy twisted beneath his grip.

"She looks like somebody's bride," he answered, and he began to snicker.

But Papa was quick about turning that laugh to a whimper. "Tell her you're sorry," he demanded, "or I'll jerk this arm out the socket."

"Sir, I think you've done that already," the boy said. "What's your daughter's name?"

He didn't even know my name. I think that's what did

it for Papa—because he didn't give the boy time to apologize. He began beating him, and the boy ran off, with Papa chasing him, furious.

And then when I knew I'd embarrassed Papa, too, then the world was too much to bear.

I wandered around the cemetery, wishing to be buried. I studied the ground, and the bones in my neck grew curved, my spine caning. I walked through the stones to the river and back, and my world was as silent as I needed it to be. It was good that I needed it to be.

And after a while, with the world so quiet, with just the crickets chirping and the toads, I began to hear voices in the nights. I'd sit up in my bed, with sliced ham on my face, the veil from Ma's dress over my head, and I'd think I'd hear her singing. I'd think I'd hear whole conversations, just faint. Sometimes I'd hear voices saying my name.

Being so lonely, it was only natural for me to track down those sounds.

So I started sleeping on Ma's grave, but the voices were always just out of reach. It was like hearing someone through a vent, someone in another room. And I wasn't sure if the voices were outside or inside my head. It took a long time to tune my ears, to cut off the outside and dive to the sounds.

Then one night, I chased down my ma's voice. She said, "Something smells like meat."

"It's me," I said. "Don't you see me?"

I took off the veil and peeled back the ham, and I saw my ma there, though it was like I saw her through a screen. I saw my ma digging mud from beneath her toenails. Ma squinted her eyes and said, "Finch?"

"Hey, Ma."

"You're here?" she said.

"I guess so," I answered.

"For good or just visiting?"

"Visiting," I answered, though I wasn't wholly sure. "Who's that crying?" I asked. "Marcus Livingston," she said. She was exhausted from hearing him already.

"Is it really that bad here?"

"Not so bad," she said. "Except I miss you," and she reached to kiss me, but there was no way. "I'm so sorry," she said. "I'm just so sorry."

"It's okay, Ma," I told her.

"You shouldn't be here," she warned, but I stayed.

"There's a price," she said. "If you borrow time here, you'll have to pay for it."

"I don't care," I told her, and she comforted me, with just words, because I couldn't reach her.

Oh, if I could have reached her, if she could have reached me. I lamented all those nights when she came to my bed, her hands on my face, feeling into my collar, tracing ridges. I wished I'd grabbed her then and held on. I moaned above her grave for the touch I couldn't feel, rolling like a cat in the dirt where grass had not yet grown.

I'M GOING TO green Finch's ivy," Lucy declares.

The workday is over. The Dead are having free time, playing poker and making necklaces with clover flowers. But Lucy's not ready to quit.

"Her ivy's green already," the Mediator replies. "And besides, it's almost dark."

"I won't be gone long," Lucy tells her. "The new leaves, they need speckling." And she darts across the graveyard, hurdling over tombstones, following me home.

I'm tired. I spent the whole day laying bricks around a war vet's grave. It was something his grandson had seen in a magazine and requested. He wanted an ugly little pen for his grandpa and sent a check to pay for the bricks, the mortar, my labor. But there is no way to charge him for the ache between my shoulders and in the middle of my back at the one place I can't reach.

"I don't know where you get all that energy," I holler to Lucy, who's now up ahead.

"I borrow it from the universe," she answers. "Didn't you take physics? Energy is neither created nor destroyed. It just changes shape. There's a law about it. It goes something like that."

"I see," I tell her. "Listen, I'm glad for the company, but when I get home, I'm going in to take a bath."

"That's fine," she says. "I'm just here to green your ivy." And she giggles to herself and does a somersault as she makes her way into my yard. She's just like a child sometimes, begging for my attention.

I go on inside and run myself a tub. I put in eucalyptus soap and lots of warm water, and I sink to my shoulders there and steep.

"Hey, Finch," Lucy calls from outside the window.

"Hmmm?" I say.

"You asleep?"

"Nah," I mutter.

"I need a favor," she whispers.

"What?" I ask. "Why *did* you follow me home?"

"I need you to talk with Mama again," she tells me, seriously now. "I need for her to know I killed myself."

When I open my eyes, I can see her in the mirror, her elbows propped up on my windowsill, framed in the ivy growing around it.

"Lucy, how many times you gonna ask me to do this?"

"Until she admits it," she says. "She's gotta admit it."

"I got one question for you: What does it hurt for her to think you were murdered? If it's easier for her to accept murder over suicide, then why do you care?"

Lucy doesn't answer me at first. I see that she's studying my body, staring at me laying there, and I almost pull the shower curtain when she catches herself.

"I'm sorry," she says. "Your scars are just so—"

"Ugly," I answer for her, and I lay my wet washrag over my burned shoulder, like it's big enough to hide me. I'd need five or six washrags to cover all I need to hide. I'd need a whole towel.

"Stop it." She laughs. "Let me see."

"No," I say, rolling my back to her.

"Finch, let me see. They're not ugly."

And so I remove the cloth and return to my back, almost defiantly, almost daring her to say the wrong thing.

"It's strange not having a body at all," she tells me. And it takes me a while to digest that, because I can only see her when

I remember the shape she held in the past. But that's about *my eyes*—not her presence.

Then she asks me, "Have you ever flown in an airplane?"

I shake my head no.

"If you ever get a chance, fly. From the air, the ground looks a lot like your skin. You wouldn't believe how intricate and detailed and beautiful . . ." and she trails off, color spreading up her face.

"Tell me about your mama," I say to get her back on track.

"Oh, I don't know." Lucy sighs. She buries her head into her arms, then looks back up, into the mirror, speaking to my image. "Do you know how many times Mama took me to the beauty parlor to get my hair teased up and sprayed, when all I wanted to do was jump on Charles Belcher's bed? Or how many times she made me walk around the house with books on my head when I wanted to play softball? I swear, Finch, it just makes me so mad.

"Do you know that I took piano lessons instead of play-ing softball because I couldn't show off softball skills to judges in an auditorium? I sat in front of lighted makeup mirrors and learned where to put the blue eye shadow and where to shade with purple. And if I got a zit, she screamed at me for eating chocolate. Of *course* I ate chocolate! And then if I gained a few pounds, she'd keep me home from school to make sure I didn't eat. If I fell off the side of my high-heel shoes, she'd make me wear them to school. It's like I did everything that she wanted—because she insisted on it—and most of it was against my will."

"I hear you," I say. "I really do. But tell me what that's got to do with hurting your mama this way. Is it really that important?"

"*Yes,*" Lucy replies. "Yes. Because the running away I *chose.*

And my life up north might not have been all that impressive, but it was still mine. And my death was my choosing, too. It might've been a bad choice, Finch. It might've been the worst one I could make. But it was *mine*."

And I want to ask her if she really thinks it matters anymore which choices were hers, which choices were not. Even I know that things happen for reasons, if you let them happen.

But she's Lucy Armageddon, and she's stubborn with my heart.

"Do you love your mama?" I ask.

"Of course I love her," she says.

VACATION BIBLE SCHOOL has just let out, and the children race down the street towards Lois Armour's house. It's her day to serve refreshments, but she doesn't do it in the Fellowship Hall like the other hosts. She's prone to seizures and afraid to leave home. So she invites the children onto her concrete lawn, one age group at a time. The punch and pound cake sit on her metal glider chair, and a small girl is pushing the chair back and forth, watching the punch slosh as Lois greets the sixth graders who've just arrived.

Her hair is bleached and loopy from rollers, her makeup on thick. She wears a sundress that clasps tight to her chest, and a little mound of fat pokes up above it in the back.

"Hey there, Aaron," she says. "How's your mama?" and ushers him in. Then she looks back to the child spilling punch. "You quit that right now, Randi Flanagan," she says.

Without transitions, she's back to her greetings, patting each child on the shoulder. "Hey, Heather and Shereen and Stephanie," she says. "Come on in."

And I'm behind the sixth graders, on my way to the store, but not willing to miss an opportunity.

Lois smiles and kisses and pinches cheeks. And just when she reaches the last child, she sees me, like a bad dream, standing behind a boy I don't recognize.

Suicide, I mouth without sound, and walk on.

I'VE HARDLY SWALLOWED my lunch and gotten none of it digested when Leonard bangs on the door.

"Well, hey there, howdy," I say. "You back for another melon?" I know why he's here, but even *I'm* surprised that Lois has done her tattling so soon.

"Finch, I got to take you in," he replies. His voice is quiet, almost apologetic, and I notice that his eyelids are puffed up like he's either slept too hard or hasn't slept in a week.

A skanky kitten leaps over from the swing onto the screen door, clawing as she climbs. She cocks her head at Leonard, like she's showing off. "Shoo," I say, and push her down. And when

I kick the door open, Leonard backs up, surprised that I came right out.

"You're jumpy today," I say.

I've got my watering tin in hand, and I make my way around the porch rail, saturating window boxes and hanging baskets until the liquid drips from the bottom.

"See this Pathos?" I show Leonard. "Would you believe it grows two to three inches a week? I'm gonna see if I can't get it to drape all the way around the porch like a window dressing. Wouldn't that be pretty?"

"Yeah," he agrees. "Finch, I ain't lying. I need you to take a little ride with me. Lois Armour's done taken out a warrant."

"For what?"

"Harassment," he says, tired. "We'll get it straightened out, but you got to come with me."

I have never ridden in a police car before, but it's nothing remarkable or exciting, neither one. Leonard's car stinks of cigarette butts. He doesn't put me in the back, though. He rides me there in the front. He turns on the radio as soon as we get in the car, but the knobs need adjusting. All the way to the station, I listen to static.

I don't get arrested. I get "a talking-to," where they fuss at me for aggravating a sick woman. I'm asked to sign a paper saying that I won't go within some distance of Lois Armour— maybe fifty yards. I can't remember the details. I'm not to call her on the phone or send her letters. And I have to sign a paper saying I understand the rules. There's a copy of the form for the police, a copy for Lois, and a copy for me. Leonard hands me a pen and I write "Lucy Armageddon" in the space where it says "Signature." The fools don't even notice. An officer named

Phillips tears it apart, hands me my copy, puts one in a file and another one in an envelope for Lois.

"You're free to go," the officer tells me. But I'm ten miles from home, with no way to travel and nobody to call. So Leonard has to drive me back. He acts irritated about it, and when he grabs my shoulder to lead me to the car, his grip is just short of a pinch.

Being touched makes me dizzy. I feel the places he fingered long after his hand has lifted. Leonard's mood is terrible, but no worse than mine, and when he turns the radio back on, I reach over and switch it off.

"It's the truth," I tell him, nearly hollering. "She *did* kill herself. And part of the reason she did it was 'cause she had no one to turn to—least of all her half-wit ma, who ain't had a seizure in years! And it's for Lois's own good that she admits it."

"Why do you care how Lucille Armour died?"

"Because she killed herself for a *reason*, Leonard."

"We don't know that she wasn't murdered."

"Read the report."

"How did *you* read it?" he asks curiously.

"I didn't. Lucy told me about it."

"Goddamn it, Finch. Would you quit that shit? Would you just quit it? Even if she did kill herself, she surely ain't talking about it now. Okay? So drop it."

We drive on for a while, passing farms and hardware stores, going over a little bridge and a bigger one, and I mutter, "She couldn't live with herself. She couldn't bear another day with the secrets she was holding."

And Leonard hits the brakes and pulls over to the side of the road just past the Tredegar County Library. The shoulder is soft and we nearly wind up in a ditch. When we've been stopped for a few seconds, Leonard speaks, without turning his head toward me and without taking his hands from the steering wheel, his hairy knuckles wrapped white around it.

"Now listen," he says. "I've had a real bad day. There's things going on you don't know. And to tell the truth, I don't give two hoots and a damn whether Lucille Armour shot herself in the head or got blasted by a pack of gypsies. My mother is in the hospital with a nervous disorder. My father is threatening to put her in a nursing home. Them cats you gave me have little white worms wiggling out their asses and falling on my bedspread. My water heater is broke, and I got the ladies' Sunday school class in a blue-headed tizzy over the bum that died a few weeks back."

"William Blott?" I ask.

"Yeah," Leonard growls. "You been talking to *him, too*?"

"Sure enough," I claim, and he shakes his head and cranks the car again. I can't tell if he's more annoyed or calming down, but then he resigns himself to a hollow laugh.

"Well, when you were talking, did he tell you he was a queer?"

"I don't believe that for a minute," I say.

"Oh yeah," Leonard continues. "He was as queer as they come. Did he tell you he paraded around in ladies' panties?"

I don't have an answer for that one.

"Did he tell you, Finch, that he was the one who was stealing women's underpants off the clotheslines back a year or two ago? Poor old Reba Baker recognized her own undergarments in his things."

"You sure he was the thief?" I defend. "There's a lot of white bras and underpants for sale at Sears and Penney's."

"Well, we can't exactly prosecute him for it, anyway, now can we?"

"Then don't accuse him."

And right when we get to the cemetery, he says, "That bastard didn't even have a house on the property. Musta had a dozen little pop-up campers back there. All of 'em old and dirty—filthy nasty. We haven't even been through his stuff. The ladies' Sunday school class went into one camper and found all their underthings, and that was the end of it."

I hurry to get out, but I can't find the door handle at first. When I finally get it open, I'm red in the face and about to start cussing.

"Shoot," Leonard says. "If you talk to William, ask him if he had anything to do with the break-ins over on China Street."

I slam the door hard and head for Lucy's stone.

THE DEAD HAVEN'T come in from their day's work, and I haven't got the energy to meet them. I wait at Lucy's grave for a bit, and then I make my way across the hill to admire the Blott memorial. It doesn't even need a tree or a shrub planted to beautify the place. It's regal all on its own.

And I'm not meaning to eavesdrop. I'm really not. I'd been thinking William was out conjuring a breeze—forgetting that he's not light enough yet to leave the surrounding area.

I'm not meaning to snoop. Most of the Dead know me already and know that while I can't reach them, I'm sometimes with them. But William has taken what the Mediator said too literally, perhaps. She's told him that the living world walks a contiguous plane. He hasn't been around long enough to learn there are always exceptions.

And so, admiring his tomb, I happen to see him holding baby Marcus in his arms, rocking. I happen to see William Blott nursing Marcus with bright blue ninnies. He's cut a spongy football in half and locked his ninnies into place with a maternity bra. And baby Marcus, who always cries, baby Marcus, who screams each time the mayor or his wife or even Leonard passes through the cemetery gates, that baby is sucking, content. He reaches up to William Blott's cheek and touches it with a small dirty hand.

THE FALLING RAIN makes the night seem cooler than it is. I usually spend damp evenings in the house, but tonight I've got things to talk over with Lucy. Already my dungarees are soppy, my shirt drenched through. And though my hair, as a rule, grows up and out like a bush, on this night, there are curls coiling in front of my eyes. I wipe the water from my face, one side smooth, one side pruned, and give Lucy an earful. "I'm telling you he had *ninnies.* And that baby was sucking."

"Did he see you?" Lucy asks.

"I don't know," I tell her. "I ran."

"Why'd you run?"

"Just because," I spit. " 'Cause what else could I do? He's a *man,* and that baby sucking . . ."

"Marcus isn't crying anymore," Lucy says.

"I know."

"I haven't heard him cry all day. It's been a long time since Marcus quit crying."

"I know."

"Maybe he died hungry, Finch. Maybe he just needed to be nurtured, and if William Blott is the one who can do that, then more power to him. Maybe now Marcus'll begin to lighten. He can't tell his story when he's screaming."

"Well, he sure can't tell it with his mouth full of ninny. Styrofoam ninny, too!"

"Finch," she calls out. "You're judging him."

"I might be, but I can't believe what I saw," and I shiver.

Then Lucy lays the blow: "You're judging him the same way people have judged you all your life."

And what she tells me makes me mad, because it's not the same thing. Not even close. "I'm *surprised,* that's all," I fuss. "You got to give me a minute to get over being surprised. I thought he was a *man.*"

"He *is* a man," Lucy says, then adds, "It's okay. You've had a shock. I've known other cross-dressers, so it doesn't upset me."

"Hmmph," I snort. I hate it when she acts high-and-mighty with me, like she's been all around the world and knows all that there is to know. I almost remind her that all the knowing she did landed her in a grave before her time, but I catch myself and unclench. I reckon she does have a point. Sometimes when the Dead piss me off, I have to keep myself from bragging that I'm alive and they're not. But it's not anything to feel superior about. Not really.

I roll over to my back and let the rain beat at my face. I

can't feel it on the thickestk scars, but I feel it on my eyelids. Rain washes the smells down off the leaves, out of the clouds. I breathe that smell, sweetly woody, and thin as a lung. In the dark, on cloudy nights, there's not much more than smells and textures. I pull a stick from beneath my back and toss it to the side.

"Your mama tried to have me thrown in jail today," I tell Lucy, readjusting with my mouth on soil so she'll hear me clearly. "I spent half the day at the police station."

"What?"

"Accused me of ha*rass*ment."

"That's insane," she says. It's what I want her to say.

"That's what I told Leonard Livingston, but he took me to town anyway. Put me in handcuffs and threw me around . . ."

"That son of a—"

"Nah. I'm kidding. Leonard's all right." I slide my lips against each other, feeling the dirt gritty there; the dirt so damp and rich and buried like a treasure in the grass; the grass tickling against my good cheek, like Ma used to tickle me with her eyelashes. "Butterfly kisses," she called them. I blink into the grass, wishing Lucy could feel those tickles. And I give her the story of what happened with her mother, without much minding anymore that I've been to jail.

"Tell me everything," Lucy begs.

"Not much to tell. Your ma was serving refreshments to the Bible school children, and she was in her front yard, welcoming them one at a time."

"She's such a hypocrite," Lucy bitches. "Won't even go to the church. If she really had the faith she claims, she'd know that church would be the *best* possible place to have a seizure. Like she's really going to *have* one."

"I stood right at the end of the line with the Bible school class. I reckon it's a good thing my spine grew crooked, 'cause I didn't look much bigger than them sixth graders. And when Lois had reached the last child, she looked up at me, and I mouthed, *Suicide,* and then I left."

"Did she cry?"

"I don't know. Last time I saw her, she was just standing there with her mouth open. Stricken. She looked stricken, I guess."

"Did she turn pale?"

"I reckon she did. A little bit."

"What was she wearing?"

"I don't know, Lucy. What difference does it make?"

"Just wondered," and she paused. "How'd you say it? *Suicide.* How'd you pronounce it?"

"Regular. *Suicide.*"

"Slow or fast?"

"Slow," I tell her impatiently. "And without a sound."

"That's good," she replies. Then, "Thanks."

Above us, there's thunder, and I ask Lucy who's working this evening, making weather on this night. She tells me that the Poet rigged it up earlier in the day. "He's got a string tied to his belt," she says. "If he rolls over in his sleep, another storm will come."

After a while, I tell her I'm going to seek cover. It's late, but I'm wanting hot tea and a shower. There's too much grit in my mouth.

"One favor," Lucy says as I rise. "Next time, tell Mama to visit."

"Your grave? You want her to come *here*?"

"Yeah," she says. "Tell her to visit next time you see her."

My bones creak and ache as I walk away. My heels hurt even though I haven't been standing. My backside throbs on each side of my spine, the clothes on my body so wet and weighing me down. When I'm on the porch, I peel them off like skins and leave them behind.

THOUGH I WAS a teenager when I found Ma in the graveyard and began to learn the ways of the Dead, I'd been exposed much earlier, just after the death of my face.

When my face had scabbed to a hard rusty shell, Ma had to scrape it with a piece of glass or Papa had to scrape it with his pocketknife—to help it heal better, they said. And while I don't remember the burning so much, I remember the scrapings, the rasping as my skin scuffed off in bloody wafers.

The doctor who came to the clinic said that the scrapings were critical. He pointed at my face as he spoke to Ma and Papa: "You have to get the scabs off to stimulate the formation of scar tissue." And he showed them how to do it, explaining that they needed to rip from different directions each time so the scars would grow evenly. That first time, it took all three of them to hold me down.

But when you are four and your ma holds a broken windowpane to your face, when you are five and your papa opens his pocketknife and rests that blade against your chin, it is almost unimaginable, that horror. I hid beneath the kitchen table, where they drug me out. I hid beneath the porch steps, where Ma chased me out with a broom.

They caught me each time and tied me down because they had to, and I screamed and twisted until the ropes burned my wrists, even before the scraping had begun. I screamed while they kissed me. I screamed while they soothed. I hardly recognized them at all. Finally, they had to shroud me in a sheet, and Ma scraped my face while Papa held my head, and I hated them for it. Though they took me out for ice cream after, or took me fishing on the river, I hated them for making that sound with my body. I didn't have much skin left, and I didn't want it torn away.

I found a secret place beneath a boxwood, and that's where I hid when I wasn't being whittled. I met the Mediator there. She came to me after the very first scraping, and she stayed with me for years.

Beneath the boxwood, the dirt was deep blue and hard, and I dug at it mercilessly, scraping into the ground to find coolness. The first time she appeared, I thought she was a queen. She crawled in on hands and knees, sat down beside me in the dirt, and offered me a stick. We dug trenches and circles and mazes in that dirt. Then she let me ring the bells on her robe until I fell asleep.

When I told my parents about my friend, they laughed and Papa said, "That's wonderful, sugar. We all need friends." They let me meet her on the grounds for games of tag, and they let me take my ribbons down to the river so she could braid my hair. When they asked me if my friend had a name, I explained that she didn't need one because she was an angel. They laughed about that, too.

The Mediator stayed with me for years, consoling me when I was inconsolable, making me see the back side of every scab. "The dead skin protects the live skin. And this tiny little scab"— and she held one on her finger—"this tiny fleck of Finch will blow away to become earth." And she'd blow the scabbed-off bits of me to the ground.

I loved the Mediator. "Where do you live?" I asked her.

"Everywhere," she said.

"Quit teasing," I'd fuss. "Where's your house?"

"Everywhere."

"Take me to your house," I begged her.

"Not yet," she told me. "It's not time."

When my arm was rotting away with infection, the Mediator was the one who healed me. I couldn't play then. I was too sick to move. The doctor said he might have to amputate. He rubbed me with ointments and told Ma to pray. I slept on the porch, on a feather mattress that we had to throw out later. And even though Papa said it wasn't my fault, it hurt my feelings when he moved my mattress downwind so that he could sit on the porch without gagging. He sat on the doorstep and read me books, pausing sometimes to get sick in the azaleas. He tried to blame it on poor digestion, but I knew.

Even though I stunk, I resented him for vomiting.

When I was sick, I couldn't play outside. And the Mediator never came indoors. Finally, she found me on the porch, and she came back late at night, when Ma and Papa were asleep just inside. In her arms, she carried heart-shaped leaves, green and already moist with dew. She spit on them one at a time and wrapped them around my arm and shoulder. She layered my neck in heart leaves to cease the rotting.

Every night, I became a plant, strong in the stem and green as any rooted thing. Nights, I dreamed I was turning to cornstalks, the hairs on my legs and arms becoming leaves, my hair turning to silks. But every morning when I awoke, I was a girl again and the Mediator was gone. Papa and Ma praised the ointment and the country air. When I told them my friend had healed me with leaves, they nodded and smiled. And soon the burns weren't new anymore, and soon I'd lived with the burns for as long as I'd lived without them.

It wasn't until I was eight or nine that they began to worry about my imaginary friend. Ma read a psychology book, and Papa called doctors. They drove me all the way to Richmond, where a man with one gold tooth determined that I was creating playmates to help me through the trauma. Brilliant, he was.

I must have been ten or eleven when she faded away. I don't recall mourning her absence, so I guess I no longer needed her. When she was gone for good, I forgot she'd ever been around.

Until I found my ma in the cemetery and began to learn the ways the next levels operated. I began listening in, and for a while, some of the recently deceased protested. Some of the new folks didn't want me to hear their stories.

"She's not supposed to be here," they whispered to the Mediator, a new one I didn't know. They stomped their little feet and made fists. "She hasn't died. She hasn't earned the right."

But the Mediator corrected them: "Oh yes. She found us herself. She's been around in one way or another since she was burned—you just never noticed. She's been around longer than you have. She's been here longer than I have. The last Mediator left me a note all about it. She *works for us*, you know?" And the Mediator winked at me and curtsied, dewdrops falling from her fingertips.

And after that, I was welcomed there completely. To hear them, I had to keen my ears, teaching myself to hear lower pitches with one ear and higher pitches with the other. I had to bottom out my ears to make meaning of their words, and even now at times the effort aches in my jaw.

Seeing them came later. I learned to multiply my vision and blur it until it softened to music. I learned to see separately at first—like two different pictures of the same moment. At the river, I'd see Papa in his boat, paddling through the water. Then I'd see beneath the water. There, hands of the Dead tipped at the bottom of a boat, pushing it along. Intuitively, I knew that the pictures were simultaneous, that the Dead were beneath Papa, that Papa paddled as they pushed. But for years, the pictures remained separate to my brain.

Then one day, I was out walking in a snowstorm. I had my face wrapped in a scarf, and I realized as I moved down the streets that I looked just as normal as anyone else. No one recognized me as burned. And so I held up my head and pretended to be like them, at home in the living world. And that's when I locked into the other way of seeing, completely by accident. I watched a group of boys digging out a Plymouth, shoveling and cussing and working like mules. Meanwhile, a group of dead children blew snowdrifts directly at the car, giggling mischievously. When I saw both scenes at the exact same time, I thought I'd reached a new plateau. Happily, I raced to the scene to help the dead children with their prank. But the boys, who could see me, of course, yelled and chased me off, and the wind blew at my scarf, and I was different and alone again, unprotected and exposed.

And I was embarrassed at my own foolishness. Snowballs whacked into my head as I ran toward home, and I felt every pelt in ways the Dead no longer have to.

I have learned from the Dead a thousand lessons that the Living should have taught me. I listened to everything in those first years. I took it all in—unless it was Ma's turn to speak.

Then the Mediator would say, "You can't be here, Finch. Go on."

"I got nothing to say that my baby can't hear," Ma'd argue, and I'd huddle in closer to her stone.

"You must leave," the Mediator insisted. "You're about to interfere."

And I considered myself rejected. I left, brooding, and sulked for days, often thinking I'd never return to the Dead. But I always returned, and in truth, I had interfered already, keeping Ma too connected to her past. It's my guess that Ma hasn't lightened because I've been around too much. How can she tell the truth when she's thinking of me?

I HAVE DOZENS OF CATS. None of them have names anymore, though sometimes I call them by their colors or textures. "Come 'ere, Yellow," or "You hungry, Callie?" or "Get down, Matty." So they have names, in a way. Names that change as they do.

I had a cat once who slept on my shoes. I called that one Shoe. Old Wilma Hedgepath brought me a litter of kittens one spring, and I called those kittens Wilma. I tend to cats and care for them, but I don't get too attached. Cats, they have their own ways. No need to impose mine.

When the weather is warm, I open the windows, and the cats come and go as they please. There's a cat door for winter, open to any animal who wants to use it—including an occasional raccoon. Some cats spend their winters by the hot-water heater, and some cats spend their winters beneath the porch.

When I sleep inside, I sleep with cats. When I sleep on the porch, I sleep with cats. When I sleep outside, there are cats nearby, but not close enough to be pillows.

The ones who want attention have to come to me. If they rub against my leg, I'll scratch their ears. But I have no patience for the forlorn ones that hang back. Wild ones are fine, and there are plenty of them that I feed. But I don't like the ones who follow me around and then run when I get too close.

They remind me too much of myself, I reckon. They remind me of the part of me that I like the least.

I had a cat once who mattered—purely by accident. I called her Flea. She cowered beneath flies. She growled at the rain and hissed at the windows when the wind blew. I thought she was funny, and I respected her ways. She'd bite and fight. She smelled like crayons because she never took care of her coat. But she never had hair balls, either.

Flea was half-wild. She'd butt her head against my leg and let me pet her for just a moment. Then she'd claw a bloody horizon across my hand. She'd slip up beside me when I was eating crackers and lick all the salt off my saltines. And she got sick. She cocked her ears and walked crooked and drooled brown foam.

I do not use veterinarians as a rule. I give the cats food and water and shelter and leave them to their fates. But Flea was special. So I called a vet and found a box and went to catch her to drive her to town. She minced my arm and screamed like Marcus Livingston. She didn't know me at all.

It took her too long to die. She did not eat and she did not drink. She did not shit, and she moaned night and day. And I cannot abide hard exits. I have seen one too many. So one night, I decided to put her out of her misery. I didn't want to be bloody or cruel, but letting her live seemed so much worse. I defined compassion as one blow to the head, from behind, so she wouldn't see it coming.

I did it with a brick, thrown straight between her ears, where her brain rested flat, bull's-eye.

But she did not die, not right away. She growled out pitiful and long and her mouth filled with blood, and her ears filled with blood as she moaned. She got up and tried to walk but fell over on the floor. I had to pick the brick back up and bash her head again. I did it right the second time, but by then it was too late for us both.

WE CHOOSE OUR truths the way we choose our gods, single-sightedly, single-mindedly, no other way to feel or see or think. We lock ourselves into our ways, and click all the truths to one.

We put our truths together in pieces, but you use nails and I use glue. You mend with staples. I mend with screws. You stitch what I would bandage.

Your truth may not look like mine, but that is not what matters. What matters is this: You can look at a scar and see hurt, or you can look at a scar and see healing. Try to understand.

FOR THE BETTER part of a year, every time I went to the store, I wondered why Reba didn't run off William Blott. She ran off all the other drunks but let him stay. He'd sit out front with the dogs, with the people waiting to use the pay phone, and he'd whittle down pieces of sticks and give them to children who passed.

"This here's a lucky stick," he'd say. Or "This here's an eel."

"That ain't no eel," little girls would shout. "That's a damned old stick, and you're a damned old possum."

"Well, missy," Blott would reply, "if you say so."

Sometimes when I was going inside, he'd call, "Sell you a magic wand for a dollar," and sometimes I'd give him one, stuffing his whittled-down stick in my pocket and throwing it out when I got home.

But whenever he got too cold or too hot or too tired, he'd make his way inside Glory Road, and for some reason, Reba'd let him stay.

To Reba Baker, preaching to a drunk was the most logical thing in the world. She chose a logic that let her pretend she was God. What else could she do and still be Reba? William Blott came in her store each day to buy beer, even after the store quit selling alcohol. He asked her every day, "Where's the beer?" and she tried to quench his thirst by testifying.

He came in forgetful. He couldn't recall that the previous owners had been chased away by Baptists who boycotted and picketed, who called the crime hot line so many times that undercover agents finally closed the store down. The previous owners were guilty of selling cigarettes and alcohol to minors. But even worse, they kept the trashy magazines in a stand next to penny candies. The Baptists put an end to all of that.

William Blott couldn't remember that the store had been closed for a solid month before it opened under new management. A lunch counter replaced the dirty-movie section. The beer cooler had been filled with deli meats and cheeses. The floors were scrubbed, the walls painted, and floral curtains coiffed above windows. Reba called her store Glory Road, and though the local rednecks had to drive a few miles to get their booze, they still bought their groceries at Reba's.

"Who are you, anyway?" William would ask her.

"I'm the owner of this place. Name's Reba. I told you that yesterday."

"Where's the beer?"

"You don't need a drink. You need the Lord. His salvation is the biggest high a man can imagine."

"The beer cooler?" he'd ask again, but sweetly. William was always gentle.

"There ain't no beer on these premises," Reba'd patiently explain. "I told you that yesterday, too. Let me fix you something to eat."

And she'd fry him an egg or a burger, extending credit until his check came.

I couldn't believe how loving and kind she was to the sorry old drunk. I couldn't get Reba to lower the price on a loaf of moldy bread!

Day after day, he'd return, still toting the empty bottle he got from somewhere else, asking for beer. Reba made sure the whole town knew she was patient and steadfast in her treatment of William Blott.

"I'm always kind to him," Reba told the newspaper reporter. "I treat him the way I'd treat Jesus if *he* came in my store, because that's what I do. I try to treat everybody like Jesus, and that way, I know I'm doing my best.

"I didn't know for a long time that William was *sick*. I just thought he was *drunk*. I didn't find out about the *tumor* for a good long while—because William is the kind of man who keeps his personal life to himself."

The newspaper article explained that Reba had gone before her Sunday school class on William's behalf: "I told those gals that I'd met a fellow who'd had hard luck and who needed an extension of Christian generosity. Some of 'em were hard to convince and we had to meet about it three or four times before we decided to take him on as our yearly Good Samaritan project. There was another idea about hugging athletes at the Special Olympics, but we decided we could do the Lord's work right here at home."

So the women signed up to have him come into their homes for supper several nights each week. They didn't turn him away if he staggered or smelled of alcohol, the newspaper said, because "Jesus in Heaven would not turn a man away."

Even the widow ladies helped out and brought covered dishes to the homes of other people. "Of course, we didn't invite him into homes where there wasn't a man present," Reba confided to the *Gazette*.

The newspaper carried the story under the title "Good Samaritans" and featured a big picture of Reba and a smaller one of the adult women's Sunday school class. The story warmed the hearts of people all around the region—particularly people who lived far enough away not to hear the gossip on the street: "He smells so strong that we had to boil vinegar after he left"; "That man ate like there was no tomorrow, and you know, I think nearly 'bout ever tooth has rotted outta his head"; "I believe he's on dope. Alvie tried to drive him home the other night after supper, and he jumped right out with the truck still running."

I heard the tales about William Blott. Every time somebody came in to perch a wreath against a stone, I got a different account of how he'd smelled or behaved.

A month or so later, the reporter wanted to interview William Blott himself. He was doing a series on "The Life of the Homeless," and he thought it'd be particularly interesting to learn how bums survived in the rural communities and small towns—without even a manhole to warm them.

"Well, he ain't homeless," Reba Baker declared. "He lives just a mile yonder down the road, where the kudzu gets so thick. He lives back there somewhere."

"I thought you took him in because he was homeless," the reporter said.

"We took him in because he's a drunk needing God's love. There's plenty of people living in fine houses who could be transformed by warm meals, Christian fellowship, and the love of God."

So the reporter decided on a follow-up story instead—after Reba told about the way William Blott repaid the class for their kindness.

"It was December twenty-third," she said. "And William came knocking at the door. I thought at first that he needed a ride to the hospital, because he was pale and trembling. But that wasn't what he'd come for. I opened up that door, and he began to sing. And he sang like an angel of God," she told the reporter. "His voice would bring chill bumps to your arms. I'm telling you, he sang every verse of 'Away in a Manger' and it just about took my breath.

"He went to every home that had welcomed him, and he sang a carol at every door."

The story got so much attention that the Richmond television station called her up in February and wanted to do a segment for their series "Hometown Heroes." But the filming got delayed, first because of snow and then because William didn't show up at the scheduled time. Reba was mad and cussed him for a week because she thought he was pulling a drunk to spite her. She cussed his name to everybody who walked through the doors.

"If this story aired on the television, think how many other churches would be inspired to help those in need," she told me as she bagged my milk and flour. "You'd think the man would have more respect for us."

But nobody saw him for a month or more. There was speculation that he'd moved away.

By the next time I saw her, Reba'd grown worried. At the checkout counter, beneath the "Need a Penny, Take One" jar, beneath the "Help Lindsey Graham Get a Bone-Marrow Transplant" jug, beneath the MS poster with pockets for quarters and the collection plate for the Humane Society, was a poster: HAVE YOU SEEN WILLIAM BLOTT? Reba'd laminated several identical copies to the black rubber roller where you lay your groceries. Instructions to inform Reba kept rolling by beneath six-packs of soda and loaves of bread.

Reba and some of her friends even looked for his house, but they couldn't find it. They weren't exactly sure who the land belonged to, and when Reba tried to walk back into the woods at the places where she'd seen William go in and out, the kudzu grew so thick and the vines were so tangled and the place was just so briery that she gave up.

"Beats all I ever seen," she told me. "That man spooks me near-bout as much as you do, Finch. I swear, I can't figure out how he goes and comes. Not a driveway on that place."

"Well, Reba, maybe he likes his privacy."

"I tell you what! If we could get him cleaned up and get him off the bottle, he'd be a good man for *you*."

"Seems to me like you're more interested in him than I am," I told her, and I lifted the paper sack to my hip and headed on home.

Reba did get a tip, at some point. One of the local boys reported that he'd seen a woman entering and leaving those woods late at night, when hardly anybody was awake. He said he'd seen a man in a black Monte Carlo stop and pick up a woman on the side of the road.

Not long after that, William Blott returned, looking weak and skinny, with hardly the energy to speak.

"Been sick," he said to Reba, and she started asking him all about the woman Toady Martin's boy had seen leaving his property late at night.

"My sister," he said.

Reba started to call the television station, but William just looked so bad. She told me later that she knew people from other communities wouldn't understand why the Sunday school class hadn't helped him when he was ill.

"What's your address?" she asked William. "We'll find you if you get sick again."

"I'm all right now," Blott said.

"Let's get you fattened up, then," Reba announced, and she helped him walk to the counter, and took her place at the grill.

Reba really *was* dedicated to the causes she took on. Nobody ever denied that. It's just that people outside her circle couldn't help feeling sorry for the Korean orphan they'd abandoned after a year of Good Samaritan love—or for the urban children who'd received letters and care packages for months but never got to visit because Greyhound didn't drop its prices until the next year's project was underway. Everybody knew that William Blott's time was limited.

We just didn't know *how* limited.

The TV station scheduled another filming for the last week

in May. But the day before the camera crews arrived, William Blott collapsed in the parking lot of Glory Road, and Reba had to call an ambulance.

So the TV station filmed the place where William Blott had fallen. They taped lots of footage of Glory Road and the community, getting shots of Reba working the register while members of the Sunday school class, all sporting matching aprons, helped customers. The video technician did a close-up of the praying hands salt-and-pepper shakers, then of Reba's hands in the same position.

"Ugh, can you believe that?" I asked the cat sitting at my feet. I'd turned on the TV to see the story everyone had been talking about. Someone had even passed out flyers telling the neighborhood when the clip would air. We'd all seen the TV crew roll in with the station's logo painted on the van. Reba's growing celebrity was no secret in these parts.

The second part of the film cut to the hospital room, where William Blott, shrunken and confused, rested in bed while Reba sat in the chair beside him. Three other blue-headed women stood behind her with their hands on the recliner's back.

The reporter asked William how he was feeling, and he mumbled something about castor oil. The camera fixed on the tubes in his nose while Reba spoke: "He's got liver trouble. He's got a tumor the size of a grapefruit. And to all the children who are watching"—and Reba began to cry—"to all the children watching, this is where drinking will get you."

The reporter said, "You're lucky to have friends like Reba Baker and these other fine women from China Street Baptist," and William Blott nodded, his stare empty as a collection plate.

He died four days later—the morning after the tape was

broadcast—and that's how Blott's son found him, a day too late.

William Blott's obituary made the front page of the local paper, along with his picture and Reba's. It glorified his reclusiveness, calling him "sensitive" and "troubled." It said he had died of a long illness, and listed his friends at China Street Baptist among his survivors.

*   *   *

"THEY WERE ALL SO NICE TO ME," William tells us. "They accepted me for who I was—even though I didn't quit drinking or claim to. Reba Baker did a lot of good for me."

And I'm thinking, Reba Baker doesn't care for anybody but herself. "I thought you said she wore on your nerves," Papa mentions. He never had much tolerance for Reba, either.

"Well, she did. She nagged me all the time about my soul and about my drinking. But in spite of that, she was my friend. She didn't make fun of me or see me as less of a person—She came to visit me in the hospital—"

"Do you know that your son gave the Sunday school class all your belongings?" the Mediator asks him.

William pauses, then answers, "Yes, I know. I didn't *have* much. And there's nobody I know of who I'd rather have my things. Those ladies might be surprised, but they were friends to me and they accepted me, even when I was drinking and using drugs. They might be a little shocked at first, but I hope they'll find something meaningful to keep. I know Reba likes music. She sings all the time, and she loved it when I sang to her. She'll take my trumpet, I'll bet. I told her once I used to play, and she wanted me to play in the church sometime."

"Did they know about your 'other personality'?" the Poet asks. He's trying to be polite about it, since William's new.

"What do you mean?" William asks.

"Did they see you dressed like a woman? Or did you just pick up that habit since you were buried?" Lucy jokes, and when she says it, I tense up in every muscle. I'm not sure what these people will say. I try to think back to whether there've been others who've been so different. We've had other races and other religions, but I can't recall another man who wears ninnies. Plus, everybody knows what a ninny-wearing man likes to *do.*

But Lucy's lightheartedness turns out to be a good thing. Everyone laughs, and even I begin to put things in perspective. So he's got a shoulder-length curly wig now. Well, it gives baby Marcus something to bat at while he's feeding. I can think that way, too, if I try. It just takes some work.

William admits that none of the Baptists knew he had a penchant for ladies' things. He says it all ladylike, more ladylike than I would ever talk. He says it like a high-society lady, and that makes everyone laugh again. But then he gets serious. "There might be some of them who have a hard time when they figure it out."

And I'm feeling a little stupid for what I said to Lucy earlier. I'm feeling a little guilty about running away when I first saw him feeding Marcus, because William Blott is nice enough. He's just like everybody else, wanting so bad to be loved, in spite of mistakes he made along the way.

"I'm hoping they don't notice," William tells us. "Maybe they'll think I had a wife. I kept those clothes separate from the ones they saw me wear. I had a bunch of campers," he explains. "I had a job at a junkyard years back, and one of the fellows there helped me drag old camper skeletons to the woods. I used each camper like a room. And the women's clothes and makeup and things are in a camper by themselves—with a little vanity and mirror. I just dressed up in that one place. I didn't go out in public. . . . Not too much, anyway," and he sounds guilty, like he might cry.

"Now, son," Ma croaks out lightly, "you don't need to be ashamed here."

"Why didn't you tell your friends?" the Mediator asks him.

"I just didn't. They were all so nice."

"I don't blame you for not telling," the Larrimore boy says. He was the newest one before William arrived. "If I'd done the things you been doing, I wouldn't admit it, either. It's sick and disgusting."

But the Mediator interrupts him. "You've got your own confessions to make," she says sharply. "And you're next."

Yeah, I think. Let's hear your secrets, Larrimore boy.

"As for you, William," the Mediator begins. "William?"

And he looks at her.

"Your sin was not dressing in women's clothes. Do you know that?" He shrugs. "Assuming that cross-dressing is not a sin, I want you to ponder what the true sin may be. That's for next time," the Mediator tells him. "Now let's hear from Mr. Larrimore."

THIS TIME, IT'S a group of girls defiling the graveyard, except they're not playing ball amid stones or racing around. They're strolling through in short skirts and heels, smoking cigarettes, their faces made up, though their bodies are still childlike. They're alternating cigarettes and lollipops, sucking on one, then the other. I turn off my lawn mower and watch them.

They stop at an old grave where the stone is flat against land and meant to mimic the lid of a coffin. We've got lots of those in the cemetery. But on this particular one, the center has been hollowed out so that the body can rise without barriers on Judgment Day. For years, I've planted daisies in the ground there, where there is no stone. The smallest girl plops down in it, like it's a bathtub, flattening the flowers.

"I'm laying right on top of Maizie Fogg," she hollers, and laughs. Then the little smart-ass turns to me, giggling. She calls, "Hey, Granny," waving.

Another one, laughing along, she waves, too. "Hey, Granny."

A bigger one tries to stare me down. She might be thirty feet away. She looks at me hard and says, "Uhg—leee," and they all snicker and whisper. The little one jumps up and they begin to walk off. The big one outs her cigarette on the stone of Melvin Hinson, the funeral home man who brought me the swing when I was newly burned. She twists it on the marble and leaves it crumpled in its bed of ash.

I abandon the lawn mower. I try to keep my cool. I tell myself that Mr. Melvin has lightened already and won't even know. I tell myself that he wouldn't care if he did. He'd laugh at the meanness of living children. He wouldn't care, and I shouldn't, either.

I tell myself that one of them could be Lucy, that all of them are probably her cousins or nieces.

The smallest one looks back. She sees me cutting across the grass and jerks her head around, leaving her yellow ponytail swinging.

Then the bigger one turns around, her thick legs spread. She puts her hands on her hips and stares at me from behind large round glasses and orange makeup that only accentuates her pimples. Already she stands too tall. I look at her and know she wishes she looked more like her friends, who will soon have waists and boyfriends, whose eyes aren't lost in the fatness of their cheeks.

"You got something to say to me?" she says hard, almost in a holler, her fists clenched.

"Yeah," I reply. "What are you doing in here?"

I think, She might hit me. I think, Remember Lucy. Remember being a teenager. Remember how lonely.

"I've come to pay my respects to the dead," she mocks, and she whispers something else under her breath. The other girls, still playing tough, laugh too high. But their laughs cut off to silence and betray them.

"Looks to me like you trying to whore for the dead, prancing around here with your ass hanging out like that," I tell her. "Is this how you pay your respects?" I hold up her cigarette butt.

She doesn't say a word

"Let me tell you about this man," I say. "You see this stone? This one here with the black spot of your *respect* on top? This man right here, he's the father of Ms. Bertie Waldrop, the principal at the junior high. What school did you say you go to?"

The big girl gets round in the eyes, the other two giggling without sound. The big one turns and heads down a path of bricks I layed myself. The hill is steep, and after rains, the mud's slick. But the bricks help you keep your balance. The girls still stumble, slowed down by the incline. The little ones keep peeking back to see where I am.

But they're too cool to run, which is what I do. I skip ahead of them and cut them off at the bottom of the hill, at a gravestone topped by an angel. The angel stands eight feet high, I reckon, and she's dark from weather, and she's half-concealed by the branches of a crepe myrtle tree I planted myself, years and years back. I was probably still in my twenties.

I cut them off, and I point to the angel, sepia-dusty and shrouded in pink flowers from the tree, and I say, "See here? This angel watches over the place. This angel's the one who told me you were misbehaving and where to find you."

The girls look up and then down and then at each other, rolling their eyes. "You crazy," the chunky one says. "We see you talking to these dead people like they can hear you."

"Oh, they can," I say. And I'm not mad anymore. In fact, I'm enjoying myself. I lead them down the road a bit, toward my house, then toward the gate.

"They ought to put you in the crazy house," one child tells me. "I'm gonna call the crazy house when I get home and tell 'em to come pick you up."

And the others laugh like it's funny.

"You see this grave here?" I say. "This one belongs to Jed Larrimore. Now, he wasn't much older than you when he crashed his car over on Bottle Branch Road. Did you know Jed? He never got to play in a single football game. Did you know he would've been on the team when school starts this year? Did you say you knew Jed?"

No answer.

"His friends bring him these little flags and stick 'em on his grave," and I pull them up and show them. "This flag's the U.S. flag, of course. And this one's for the U.S. Navy, because Jed had dreams of commanding a whole fleet. Course, he never made it to the navy. It's nice of his friends to bring him the flags, don't you think?"

They've increased their walk to a trot, but I'm quicker. I stay ahead of them and point out things all the way to the exit.

"You taken history classes yet? Here's a history lesson for you. Engraving methods have changed in lots of ways throughout the years. But if you'll look right there, you can see that on a real old stone, the engraver left the letters and chipped the stone away, so that the words poke out. But on newer stones, the words are actually engraved *into* the marker.

"When you get buried, you'll probably have your names carved into the stone. You ever thought about what you want on your stone?"

They keep moving, expressionless.

"Well, have you? 'Cause if you've got a favorite Bible verse, you can get that put on it."

"We ain't religious," a child declares.

"That's all right. There's plenty of nonreligious folks out here. In fact, there are some grave markers in the shapes of trees and scrolls and even obelisks. Now this one here—this is Miss Sadie Witherspoon. She *was* religious. She spent twenty years as a missionary to Kenya, doing her best to help others. I wish you could've met her. I heard her tell one time about seeing a wild elephant pick up a man in his trunk and bash him into a tree. She always regretted that she couldn't help him." My voice has lifted to almost a song, loud and clear and proud to know these people. I could tell these girls stories all day long.

The children have quit trying to run off and now keep their pace with mine.

"And this one belongs to a baby who died at birth. Isabel Jenkins would've been her name. Don't you just love the little ones? I love the stones with little lambs or angels. Here's another one," and I point. "Roland Ashworthe Jenkins. Two dead babies in one family. I can't imagine naming a baby Roland, can you?"

They don't answer me. "See here," I say, "if you could be buried anywhere on these premises, where would you want your stone to be?" Then I just stop and stare at them. And when the silence goes on too long, I leave it.

"Why are you *doing* this?" one of the girls asks, and her voice is way too loud, and she begins to cry, ducking behind a tree to hide her face.

"Look," the big one says, now tough again. "You made her upset."

"I just thought if you wanted to pay your respects, you ought to understand why these people deserve it. They deserve respect, you know? And one day when you're buried here, you're gonna hope some little tramp don't come along and put out her cigarette on your tombstone."

"We can walk in here if we want to," the middle-sized one shouts, and she's just a brat, a regular brat, not as impenetrable as she was pretending to be.

"You're *welcome* in here," I tell them. "It's a good place to come to quiet your mind. But I expect you to behave yourselves. Okay?"

They just stand there.

"Okay?"

And they nod.

"Next time you come, you find me. I'll show you some things you ain't seen before."

I usher them out, laughing to myself. Behind me, I hear one of them holler, "Uhg-leeee," fierce again, now that she's got her distance. It doesn't bother me. I know that their mouths say things their hearts don't mean.

THE MEDIATOR IS PRACTICING ballet on the lawn mower as she waits for me, the grass heavy all around.

"You did that very well," she says, stretching her leg on the crossbar of the handle.

"Thank you."

"I didn't realize you were so good with children."

"I'm not."

"Sure you are," and she twirls on her toes on the red metal edge, takes a bow, and hops down.

I clap for her, and she turns and begins clapping for me. All around, I hear clapping, from the Dead, and in the distance, Lucy's piercing whistle.

"Bravo," the Mediator says. "You're coming right along."

I'm not sure what she means by that, and I'm a little embarrassed to have been watched. Sadie Witherspoon comes up and congratulates me, too, but she's very light and can't make herself apparent for long. Which is a good thing. I hurriedly pull at the cord to crank the machine back up.

I mow the back side of the hill, up to the top. William Blott sits beneath a tree and points out things in the ground to Marcus Livingston. I'm glad he's lightened enough to move around the area. It's a good sign for him. Soon he'll be going everywhere.

William waves to me awkwardly, like he's not sure I can see him on a regular afternoon, but he smiles when I wave back.

Then Marcus waves, his hand turned out this time, instead of in.

Later, while they're napping, I take a lily and plant it at William's tomb. A peace offering, though he doesn't know there was ever anything wrong.

PERPETUAL CARE ISN'T cheap. There's money needed for gas and upkeep of the mowers. It costs to keep the roads safe, and every spring I have to fill in potholes where water froze in cracks and exploded the pavement. There's the cost of maintaining a secure fence, and the price of proper drainage. And though I make my money from the funeral home, which pays to bury the bodies on this land, each year I send out collection envelopes to the families of the people residing here.

I type up a letter and copy it at the post office, inviting living family members to come and enjoy the tranquility. I mention that there are four benches positioned beneath shade trees, that there's a view of the river and a view of the church and of the whole neighborhood from the top of the hill. I remind them that the hours are from eight to six, and I ask them for twenty dollars to pay for the upkeep of their relative—more if they have it, less if they don't.

I get pretty good results. There's a lot of people who appreciate knowing that their loved ones are being watched over. You won't find year-old plastic flowers faded by the sun. You won't find old poinsettias left to brown and wilt. You won't find foot-stones hidden beneath weeds or whole plots gone to ruin. Not here. Not while I'm in charge.

For a nominal fee, the families can request special services. For twenty dollars, wildflowers planted over their loved ones' plots. For fifty, a fruit tree. For two hundred, a whole backdrop of shrubs. But most of the families don't go this far. They know if they wait long enough, there's a good chance I'll plant a seed for their relative for free.

To the families who've lost relatives in the past ten years, I write notes. "Best wishes to your family," and "May your grief become more bearable with each passing year." Back and forth between those two, a personal touch, though impersonal—a trick I learned from Papa.

"You've got to treat 'em like they're some*body*," he said. "'Cause they *are* somebody—even if you don't know 'em from Adam."

"It's a lot of work," I told him. He was in a wheelchair by then, and I was running the cemetery by myself. He was simply overseeing at that time.

"But it's work worth doing," he insisted.

So I wrote the notes as he studied my hand. "Best wishes to your family," and I signed them, "Finch Nobles."

"You got to write so they can read it," Papa used to fuss.

"I can't help it," I argued. "That's how I write."

"Well, I don't care if you have to print, you write it so they can read it," and he'd add, "This is a *business*. You do what you have to."

I stuff each envelope, lick it, and put it in a pile. A cat I've never seen before keeps guard over the stack. Another cat sits on the stamps and whines when I move him.

I address each envelope carefully, with ink that doesn't run. The one to Lois Armour on Glass Street holds my attention for a long time. I pull it out of the stack.

"Should I do it or not?" I ask the cat. But the cat ignores me. I rip the envelope in two, take up another copy of the letter, and begin again: "May your grief become more bearable with each passing year. May you come to admit that your daughter killed herself, and may you stop pestering the police about arresting black boys who had nothing to do with her death. Best wishes to your family."

It looks good to me when I read it. At Lucy's request, I add, "Come soon for a visit," and then I sign, "The Management," to comply with the restraining order. I mail it out along with all the others.

I'M CANNING WHEN the phone rings, and I almost don't answer it because I'm bogged to my elbows in stewed tomatoes. The only people who ever call of an evening are boys in faraway states trying to give me a credit card. But sometimes it's nice to hear about the weather in Idaho.

"Hello?"

"Finch? Leonard. Turn on the news," and the line clicks.

I wipe my hands on an old dishrag and pull out the button to start the TV. It takes a long time to get past the static, and though there's no picture yet, I can hear the anchor say, "Coming up next—the woman we've come to know as the Good Samaritan—disillusioned."

"And," the other anchor adds, "ways to get rid of those old tires you've been saving in your garage. All this and more when we come back."

I wrestle with the rabbit ears all through the commercials until I can make out the picture, and by the time I get tinfoil wrapped around the tips, I see words flash across the screen: "Kindness—At What Price?"

They review the story of Reba Baker and William Blott, even replaying bits of footage from the earlier taping. Then the camera pans a wooded area that looks more like a junkyard than anybody's home. All around, pop-up campers and shells from pickup trucks and even a couple of little pull campers are sprinkled and wedged between trees and scrub. There's a stove and an old sewing machine with colorful fabric draped across, a line hanging from the trees, and fancy costumes pinned up.

Then the camera turns to Reba, who is scratching her arm. She notices the microphone and begins to speak, the tears already falling: "We were given all William Blott's belongings by his son after he died, and we were planning on using them for the youth of the church. We were led to believe that we could turn his house into a club for our boys and girls, and this is what we find."

She spreads her arms around.

"Trash and sinfulness everywhere. He was the one who'd been stealing our underclothes off the lines, and there's a whole trailer full of ladies' things right there." She points to a pop-up camper.

"And there are perverted sexual magazines and objects so vile that I cannot say them on the television; I would not have those nasty words in my mouth."

The reporter tries to calm her, saying, "Ms. Baker, is there any chance that you'll be able to salvage or sell any of his things? There do appear to be valuables on this propery. The antique vanity, for instance. Or the musical instruments?"

"I would not *touch* his *filthy* belongings. Our church will not be tainted by his sinful, lustful ways. Do you see that commode?" and she points to it, sitting between two pines. "He'd been *using* it out here, not even connected to a septic tank!" And she begins to cry again, scratching at the skin above her eye. "When the Lord is ready for us to have a clubhouse for the children, he'll send us one. The Lord would not insult us this way." And Reba buries her face into the crook of her arm. That's where the tape ends.

"As you can see, Blott's legacy is not what it appeared," the reporter says to the anchors. "I've talked with lots of the other members of the Sunday school class, Curtis and Lynda, and they echo Ms. Baker's sentiments exactly."

"Did you get any comment from Mr. Blott's son, who gave Ms. Baker this property?"

"We tried to speak with him today, but he had no comment.

It's worth mentioning that he'd had no contact with his father since infancy."

"It's certainly heart-wrenching to see someone like Ms. Baker, who does so much for her community, so broken by these circumstances," one of the anchors says.

"You have to wonder if she's not overreacting a bit," the other anchor adds.

"She *did* say that she'd do it all over again," the reporter tells them. "And the adult women's Sunday school class at China Street Baptist Church out in Tredegar County will begin a new Good Samaritan project in the near future. But Ms. Baker's plans for this land and for Blott's belongings are, and I quote, 'to set a fire so hot, it scorches the evilness out of the air.'"

I click off the TV and try to call Leonard back. But I don't have his number. The operator gives it to me, and he answers on the second ring.

"Meet me at Blott's land," I say.

"What?"

"Meet me there. I don't know how to find his campsite."

"I'm in for the night," Leonard says. "I don't feel good. I'm not going back out."

"Then tell me how to find it."

"You won't be *able* to find it, Finch. It's almost dark, and it's way back in the woods, plumb hidden back there."

"Have you been?" I ask him.

"Yeah."

"Then I'll meet you at the big curve in twenty minutes."

THE TRUCK I drive used to be Papa's. It's big and blue, a Chevy, with round hips over the back tires and places to stand on the sides, like a fire truck. I check the toolbox to make sure I got my good flashlight, climb in the cab, and I'm off.

My truck clanks and jolts. Nobody can drive it anymore but me—not even the mechanic—because there's a special way you throw the gears. But I love my truck and plan on keeping it for a while if the floorboard doesn't rust through. I've reinforced the floor on the passenger side with a piece of plywood, then pulled the carpet back over it so that it can pass inspection. And all across the dash, I've got dried flowers and bits of stick and bone. There's a cat's tail I found chopped off by some sort of blade. I've tied a string to the end, and it hangs from the rearview mirror, dangling tabby. It swings slow, because slow's the way I drive.

When I get to the curve near William Blott's place, there's nobody around at all, and the night so dark, it looks like the whole world's just an echo of something bigger. I pull over to the shoulder, get out, and jump the ditch.

I wait around for Leonard, but not for long. Then I begin walking the stretch of road, looking for shoe prints and bent-over grass. If a camera crew has been in those woods, and all those church ladies, and a reporter, I know I ought to be able to find the path they made.

And I do. It takes me a while, but I do.

I follow the trampled way for a while and even still, there are briers sharp as blades and long, like nails, that catch in my hair and my clothes. They scratch worse than cats as I pass through. There is kudzu wrapped around every tree, like a logic, swallowing up what shrinks inside. It's a jungle of a world, in July, wild and looming, and it's not long before I lose sight of the slight path I'd found. It'd be easier in daylight.

Briers claw at my socks and vines catch beneath my chin. I feel like I'm trying to walk through a hammock, and I have to swim with my arms and twist to get through bushes. I cuss Leonard with every breath. My light is good, but the woods are dense, and one little shining isn't enough. I wish for a miner's hat with a spotlight attached.

Finally, I reach a place where the vines seem woven together like a wall. I push against them with my hands, and though they are flexible, they do not give. I realize I'll have to climb over, and so I shine my light upward to see how high. At the top of the viny fence, briers stretch two rows thick, like barbed wire.

At first, I'm stunned, and then I'm tickled when I realize William Blott had built a fortress for himself, taming nature just enough to afford him protection.

I drop to my belly and wiggle beneath, just like the children who come onto the cemetery grounds without permission.

And then I'm in. I dust myself and circle the place with the flashlight. It looks as if those campers had to be dropped from the sky, with the living fence forming boundaries all around. They must have been there for years for the woods to grow up around them that way. I work the perimeter with my light, shining on the overgrowth and shining on the campsite. At the opposite side of my entry, I see that somebody has broken through the fence with a hatchet or scythe. They've made a rough door for the camera crews and ladies, but they didn't bust through the top levels of briers.

But the inside is miraculous—like being inside somebody's head. It feels like a privilege to see it all.

There's a camper shell designed to fit onto a pickup standing upright and supported from behind by two pine trees. William Blott has made a clothes rack in that camper shell, using a young sapling stripped to its trunk as the bar. He's slipped the narrow tree through holes on either side, and his clothes hang on regular hangers, here in the woods.

There are other clothes on a line—costumes and boas and sequined gowns swinging from the rope, just above the dirt, like ghosts. His bras appear to be different sizes, and it startles me to see them hooked around sawed-off stumps. In the night, with just the light shining in one place at a time, it's like headless nymphs wear those bras. I discover them individually, behind me, ahead, to my side. Each one makes me jump.

There's a small pull camper, no bigger than a horse trailer, and when I see that it has no door, I lean inside and shine the light around. It's his bedroom—complete with a bed, though dirty and unmade. I shine my light on a nest at the far corner of the crumpled bed, and then a bird comes flying at me, black and squawking. I lunge and fall against the camper's moldy side, jostling it hard. And inside, an alarm clock falls and begins to ring.

Before I know it, I'm on the other side of the campground, my back against a tree, swallowing to keep my heart from jumping out my throat, the ring piercing my ears.

And in the dark, I hear a rustling, then "Yo," a voice calls from deep in the woods. "Finch? You in there? What the hell's going on?"

It's Leonard, and I catch my breath and shine my light in the direction of the sounds of feet crunching through moss and mulch. He comes in through the door in the fence, dressed in coveralls and a cap, though the evening is hot. It's clear he's been here before.

"It's just a clock," I tell him. "I knocked it over."

"You wanna turn it off?" he growls.

"No," I say, and he nods and chases down the sound.

The bird comes flying at him, too, and he runs out saying, "God Almighty damn. Why didn't you tell me there was a bird? Are you laughing?"

"I thought you weren't coming," I answer, ignoring his questions.

Then he points to a camper I haven't been in. "You seen this yet?"

I shake my head.

"Come on." He leads me to a pop-up with a beaded entranceway, and when I push through, it's like something you'd see in a movie. It's got red poofy pillows with tassles and a daybed covered with silky sheets. There's the dressing table with makeup still sitting out, little sponges in the shapes of triangles darkened with the liquid. My flashlight hits the mirror and bounces off, and in the reflection, I can see the shelf along the top lined with wigs and foamy ninnies.

I do not wear makeup myself. There was never any chance I could cover up my faults, and so it seemed pointless to bother with painting my lips. But being in William Blott's dressing room makes me feel little and silly, and there's a part of me that wants to do my face.

"Creepiest thing I've ever seen," Leonard says. "Let's go." He trips over a pair of heels, massive and gold. I take a tube of lipstick, stick it in my pocket, and follow Leonard through the streaming beads. "What're you doing here anyway?" he asks, leading me to the hole in the living fence.

"Collecting William's valuables," I say. "And don't you try

to stop me, neither. If Reba's got plans to burn this place—and you know that she just might—then I'm gonna take some of his things back to his grave."

"You are *not*," Leonard tells me. "If I have to put you in handcuffs, you're not taking things away from here. We're leaving. We're leaving *now*."

And he walks on out into the woods, but I dip behind another camper and then inside. This one's full of books, and most of them stink like mold. I pick up a book of photographs— photographs of misfits—and the pages are warped from rain or other liquid.

"Finch?" Leonard calls, looking for me. "Damn it, you've seen it now. Come on."

"I ain't done looking," I tell him. "And I ain't leaving. I found my way in without you and I reckon I can find my way out."

He shines his light in the doorway and says, "Well damn. You wouldn'ta thought the fellow'd been a reader, would you?"

And there are books on the ocean and marine biology, books of poetry and books of art. There's a whole set of encyclopedias and a bunch of books he'd written in with a pen, but they've all suffered water damage. I have to peel the pages apart, and even then the writing has run together, words layered over each other like skins.

There are books on photography, but they're in another trailer, this one divided into two parts. In one half, there are cameras and tripods and lots of pictures, some in frames and some loose. There's a bathroom in this camper, but it looks like William used it as a darkroom. Pans of chemicals line the bottom of the bathtub, and when Leonard tries to turn on the water, nothing happens.

"Beats all I ever seen," Leonard says. "He's got a bathroom right here and don't hook it up to the water."

"There's no water pump out here," I tell him.

"How do you know?"

"He said so. Said there's a creek running somewhere nearby, and he brought in water in five-gallon buckets and boiled it."

"When'd he tell you that?" Leonard asks suspiciously.

And I recognize my mistake. Too late. "A couple of days ago," I admit.

"Awww, Finch, damn it. We were having such a fine time," and Leonard grumbles up his face and heads out.

"Wait a minute," I call to him, because I've just seen something else. In the other half of the camper, my light shines on William's music: sheet music and a stand, a violin and a horn of one kind or another. I pick up the horn and blow it flat.

"Get that thing outta your mouth," Leonard scolds. But I just keep on blowing. I play him a medley.

"Can you believe Reba Baker wouldn't sell this stuff?" he asks. "That's ridiculous, if you ask me. It could be cleaned. Some of those children from the high school could use these instruments."

I hand him the horn, put the violin in its case, drape a camera around my neck, and grab a handful of his pictures. I can't even see them good in the dark, since they're black and white, but I take them anyway—as mementos.

"Now can we go?"

"Soon," I tell him. "Go ahead and set that down."

I wander around behind this trailer and find an old RV, a small and ancient one. The hood is missing, and when I shine the light inside, I see that William Blott has built a fire pit for cooking right where the engine used to be. It's tightly lined with stone, and in the bottom, pieces of charred wood cross ash. There's a metal dowel stretched from side to side and a small cast-iron pot with something hardened in the bottom.

"Hungry?" I ask Leonard. Inside the RV, Blott has a dining room, with a small Formica table and two chairs.

"Who do you reckon sat in that other chair?" Leonard wonders, but I don't take a guess. I'm searching through the cabinet, looking at cans of beans. William must not have eaten anything else. No wonder he liked Reba.

There's water stored in plastic jugs around the edges of the room, and dust covers everything, even the cobwebs—or maybe it just looks that way in the artificial light.

"Hard to believe," Leonard says.

"It really is," I agree. "He said a friend helped him drag in these campers years back, but it must have been a lot of years. I hate for his stuff to burn."

"The man's dead," Leonard reminds me. "He won't know the difference."

"You got *half* of that right," I say.

We stand in the middle, looking around, just staring out at the place.

"It's amazing," I tell him. "You'd half-expect to find a circus nearby."

"Reminds me of gypsies."

"I'm taking this stuff," I tell him, pointing to the pile I've made.

"I don't like it," he says.

"She's really gonna burn it, ain't she?"

"Plans to," Leonard tells me. "She's gonna burn it off and clear it and then build a Christian park. His land goes all the way back to the road. He only used a part of it."

We walk over to the costumes draped on the line one last time, and I pull down a boa and throw it around my neck. The feathers have been wet and dried, and now they're more itchy than fluffy, and matted, like a cat too fat to clean its back.

There's a small tree behind the clothesline where William hung his hats. Fancy Sunday hats for ladies and railroad-worker hats. Even a ten-gallon hat. There are hats on every branch. I pull down a cowboy hat and stick it on Leonard's head. He takes it right off, but he's laughing.

I grab a lady hat with flowers and a veil, and I chase him down and crown him. It's too small, but I push him to the mirror, which is nailed up to a tree, and I show him what he looks like. I shine the light on the mirror, and he looks nice.

Leonard finds a New York cloak and drapes it around my shoulders, holding his hands there for a minute. We stand in front of the mirror that way, with me cloaked and boaed and Leonard hatted and holding my shoulders, his fingers grazing my neck, one side burned and one side smooth.

I tell him, "William Blott's gonna be so sad."

I tell him, "William Blott thought Reba loved him back."

I tell him, "William Blott can make baby—the babies stop screaming," remembering just in time that Marcus is Leonard's brother.

But he says, "The babies scream?" Then adds, "Don't tell me that stuff, Finch. I don't wanna hear."

We leave sad, me and Leonard both. He carries the horn and the camera. I carry the pictures, the violin, the sequined dress.

T AKE THE BABY and go," the Mediator tells me and Lucy. "Marcus doesn't need to see William this way."

Marcus is already crying, a throaty whimper. Lucy has to carry him. But I'm the one who's been instructed to soothe him. Papa volunteered me. He reminded the Mediator that after the scrapings, he always took me out for a treat, and it always made me feel better, even if the burns still hurt.

But I beg to differ. The treats were distractions. Loving gestures, yes—but not comfort. I still felt the same way at the Tastee-Freez licking a vanilla cone. I still felt the same way with a fishing pole in my hand. And I know that Marcus will not be comforted, either. Not by anything I can do. I beg to be released from this assignment, claiming that I'm no good with babies. I never wanted my own and still resent my body for putting me through the monthly pains, year after year. I remind the Mediator of how unmotherly I am, but she pays me no attention.

Just my luck, I think. When my body begins to relax, relieved that it's almost too old for the task, I get a baby shoved at me, a baby I can't even carry or hold. Like I know how to talk to a baby.

"Finch, go play with him," Papa coaxes.

"But I can't pick him up," I remind them.

"How tedious," the Mediator answers, and pulls down her eyebrows to let me know her disdain. "Lucy, go with her. Take the baby and go."

Marcus cries and screams and reaches his pudgy arms toward William Blott, who is balled up on the hillside, his head buried in the root of a tree, crying as if his lungs host flames. The Mediator has her hand on his back, and Papa's there, too, saying, "Boy, you got to get yourself together."

We head out, hurrying, and Lucy asks, "What happened?"

And I say, "I'll have to tell you later," and roll my eyes toward the baby.

"Somebody didn't like somebody else's lifestyle?" she tries vaguely.

"To say the least," I answer. "You see that smoke?" and I point.

She shakes her sad head and adjusts Marcus to her other hip. We walk together, down the hill to my house, and the farther we get from the graves, the harder he screams.

"I'll get him some spoons and let him dig in the dirt," I holler above him. "That's what Ma used to give me to play with."

So Lucy puts him down at the edge of the garden and tries to show him how to push up dirt with his hands, calling, "Marcus, Mar-cus" in the sweetest voice she can muster. But he just gets madder by the second.

I run up the doorsteps and into the kitchen, grab a couple of spoons, and hurry back out.

"I think he's got dirt in his eyes," Lucy tells me, and sure enough, there are streaks of mud forming on his face, between the dirt and the tears, and he's rubbing the balls of his fists against his eyes, his whole face red as a maple. I feel so sorry for him that I reach to wipe his face with my shirttail and run my hand right through his little head.

"Shit," I say.

"I'll do it," Lucy offers, but Marcus bites her.

So Lucy nurses her hand and Marcus screams and I stand there jingling spoons, making a rhythm, making them dance like tap shoes, calling, "Mar-cus. Look, Marcus." I play carnival. I try to put on a show. I kick my legs and click my spoons, but the only one I entertain is Lucy, who laughs in spite of Marcus's wailing.

"You dance pretty good for somebody who never had lessons," she teases.

I collapse on the ground, breathless. Lucy takes a spoon, and I take one, and we dig trenches all around him, plowing up dirt.

"Let's play grave digger," Lucy says, and we begin to scoop out a hole, and I try to involve Marcus, asking him to get us a dead cucumber to bury, but he just keeps screaming, his little chin quivering between bellows.

"Marcus? You can be the preacher if you want," I tempt. "You can be the song leader, or you can say the prayer." But he isn't interested.

Lucy gets up and carries him to the cucumber row and helps him pick one.

Then we bury it with full honors, Lucy trumpeting out Taps, her hands forming a horn over her lips.

"Dearly beloved," I say. "We have gathered here today to bury this cucumber named Harold."

Marcus lets out a hard-rollicking scream, and Lucy says, "This isn't working. Let's take him for a drive. That's what Mama did with me when I had colic."

"We don't have a car seat for a baby."

"Finch, he's dead," she reminds me. "It's okay."

So we get in the truck, Lucy and Marcus and me, and I circle the cemetery. He quiets down considerably after that, but as soon as I drive out in the community, he begins to cry again.

"Stick his head out the window," I tell Lucy. "Let him get some air."

So she holds Marcus by the hips, and I step on the gas, and we cruise for a while. I wave to every car I pass, because they're all staring at me, thinking I'm talking to myself, I reckon.

All the dogs bark at us, and we laugh when the pit bull that guards the corner of Crabtree and Stanley whelps and cowers as we pass. Even baby Marcus gets a kick out of that.

We drive down Glass Street, and Lucy catches a glimpse of her place and asks me to drive down the alley, too, in case her mama or daddy is out back. "I can't," I tell her. "I wish I could, but if I get caught in your yard again, I'm going to jail."

"You ever been down that alley?" she asks me.

"Well, sure," I say.

"We used to have a baby pool back there—right at the back of the yard. Me and Charles Belcher played in it for a hundred summers, it seems like. I guess you don't remember it?"

"No," I say, but I smile at her memory. It's nice to see Lucy having a good one.

"I loved summers. I didn't take a bath all summer long. I played in the water every day."

I turn down Meadow Lane and wave to the preacher's family, who're painting their house bright yellow. I drive out by Glory Road.

"See there?" I show Lucy. "A renovated joint. I don't know what happened to all the hoodlums who used to hang out there. Moved on, I reckon, after Reba Baker took over."

"My daddy used to go there after work to shoot pool," Lucy says.

"You can bet he's not doing that now."

She pulls little Marcus back in, and the wind seems to have thinned his anger, and he sits on her legs for a while just looking. It's been a long time since Marcus has ridden in a truck, I guess.

We ride out toward William Blott's land, where the smoke is so thick that I have to turn on my headlights. There are trucks parked along the highway, including some fire trucks, and it looks to be such a cluster that I turn before I get to the place where I entered the woods.

"I came out here last night," I tell Lucy. "After the late news ran a story about William. Reba Baker talked hard," I say.

She nods.

"She talked *hard*. So I figured somebody better get a thing or two that mattered to him—before it was too late."

She nods again.

"Leonard helped me," I tell her, and she looks at me cross. "He's not all bad, old Leonard."

But Marcus begins to whimper when I mention Leonard's name. So I quit talking about him. Lucy doesn't want to hear anyway, and I can't blame her. I've tainted her notions of Leonard Livingston, talking bad about him for years and holding old grudges. I even found a way to blame Leonard for letting her mama think she was murdered—and we both know that Lois Armour would have found a way to do that on her own.

"You ought to give William his things," she says. "Maybe he'll feel better if you give him his things."

"Maybe," I say. "But the damage is done."

We pass the post office and the medical clinic, and I wave to the Vegetable Man, who's making rounds in our town today. "I got a lot of respect for Blott now," I tell Lucy. "He had his own way of doing things."

She nods.

"He had a whole other way of seeing the world. Did you know he liked to take pictures?" "No," she says quietly, Marcus sleeping against her lap. Then I make a mistake. On the way back to the cemetery, I drive past the house where Marcus grew up, the house where his parents still live, and he jerks awake suddenly and begins to tremble—like a washing machine with a load too heavy. His eyes fill up with tears, his little lip poking out.

"Look," Lucy says.

"What's the matter with him?" I ask her. "Marcus?"

But he doesn't respond, and he doesn't make a sound. He just shakes and cries silently. "Oh shit," I say. "I took him by home. You think he misses his family?"

"I don't know," Lucy says.

The minute we turn off his street, he's bellowing again. He cries all the way back to the cemetery. He cries until my nerves are just jagged and it seems like all his crying, like all the crying I've heard him do for years, is coming at me at one time. His howls echo off the metal ceiling of the truck, diving hard into the windshield, like a bird that doesn't recognize glass. He cries reckless and doesn't care, looking right in my face, like he expects me to do something.

"What?" I ask him.

He furrows his brow deeper, too deep for a baby. I don't know how a baby can even do that. "What can I do for you? If you can't tell me, I can't do it." He screams out, still looking my way.

"What?" I scream back finally, loud to drown him out.

"Finch," Lucy scolds. "He can't help it if he can't talk." She hugs him like he needs protecting from me, when I couldn't hurt or help him neither one—not even if I wanted to. She's just jealous about Leonard, and I know it. Lucy's never liked Leonard at all.

Out the side of my eye, I can see that baby looking at me like I'm his only hope. And he's deafening me with his hollering.

"I don't know how to help you," I tell him, and turn my head away from them both. When I drop him back off at his plot, I tell the Mediator, "I don't know how to help him."

And later when I'm trading with the Vegetable Man, when he's pulling up my onions, I ask him, "You got children?"

"I got great-grands," he says proud.

"You ever had one cry on you for hours at a time?"

"Well, shore," he tells me. "They do that when they're teething. You give 'em a turnip," he says. "A big one they can't swallow. Something hard to chew on like that, it'll quiet 'em down."

"You got any turnips?" I ask him.

"Yeah," he says. "But you ain't got no baby, do you?"

"I'm watching a friend's," I tell him.

So we swap onions for turnips, and I take them to Marcus's grave. I arrange them in a circle around his stone.

THIS IS ALL I got," I tell William Blott. "It's all I could tote. I hope it helps." But he's not interested in the load I've dropped inside his tomb.

"You want me to arrange it for you?"

Still no answer. And I'm getting fed up with these Dead. Marcus, who screams but won't tell me what he wants—and now William, who slumps and broods, his silence heavy like the cloud of smoke that follows a hydrogen bomb. I am tired of not getting answers.

I lean the pictures up against the walls. There is one of a toothless woman making a bowl from clay, another of a man with one arm, standing beneath the awning of a barn. There's a picture of a woman, swaddled to a stretcher, stomach down and playing a keyboard with her tongue.

The pictures aren't even exceptional. They are blurred and out of focus, overdeveloped and underdeveloped, softened and streaked by rain, and I'm amazed that I can touch them at all. I am dead weary and suddenly I just want to go to a movie where the pictures are crisp and in color, where everything gets settled in just a matter of hours. I don't even want to talk to Lucy or the Mediator, who've gone about their work now, leaving William to grieve, Marcus to cling to his legs and hiccup.

I lean the violin in one corner and sit the horn on the stone that notes his dates of birth and death. I don't know what to do with the dress. I lay it on the ground like a rug, but it looks funny that way. So I pick it up.

"Do you want this dress?" I ask him.

No answer.

"You know, I was up half the night getting these things. You *could* say thank you."

No answer.

"Fine," I say. "I'm leaving." I take a deep breath and turn away, the dress still thrown over my shoulder. I don't even know where the nearest movie theater is, but that's where I'm going. To the movies. Right now.

"Thank you," William calls weakly. Then he adds, "Is the dress your size?"

"Oh," I say, and walk back to leave it with him.

"You wear it," he says sadly. "I don't need it here."

I DON'T GO TO the movies. I call up Leonard Livingston, who is working. I know he's working. I don't want to talk with him. I just want to hear his voice. His phone rings and rings, and then a machine picks up, saying, "Hello, this is Officer Leonard Livingston. I cannot take your call. Please leave your name and number and a brief message and I'll call you right back. Thank you."

Then it *beep, beep, beep, beeps*, and I hang up.

"You like this dress?" I ask a cat, a white one without a tail. I pick the cat up and kiss its head. "You smell," I tell it. "Whose trash you been eating?" I toss it on the sofa.

I pull off my dungarees. They are brown from two days' dust, with thorns still in the cuffs. I unbutton my summer shirt and stand before a mirror, in just my baggy white drawers, my white socks that poof gray about my ankles. I look like a freak show, standing there, long bones in my legs, skin beginning to give, narrow hips, but a potbelly and ninnies that fall to the edge of my rib cage because I have never worn a bra. My ma told me never to hang a bra on a clothesline, and I've never been interested in wearing one wet or dirty.

I've got arms brown to the shoulders from sun, and skin like a road map, like a map of a mountain range on my left side—my left arm, collar, neck, jaw. Even my ear looks cracked. I tie down my hair with a bandanna each morning, but the humidity resurrects it, and now, freed, it waves horizontal in dark brown frizz, floating just above my shoulders.

A cat jumps onto my back, climbing to my collar, the scarred one with fewer nerves, so that I hardly feel her claws at all. Maybe she isn't using them. She climbs up to my head and begins to knead as I get dressed. I have to push her away.

I step into the sequined gown. It's mermaid green and shimmers silvery in spite of its age. From the outside, you'd never guess that the lining is yellow and stained. I zip it up the side, reach in and adjust my ninnies. I look almost pretty when I stand sideways, though even sequins don't make up for my lack of a waist.

My hair needs tying back, and there are bread bags in the kitchen. I go there to get a twist and find myself on the phone again, listening.

"Hello, this is Officer Leonard Livingston . . ."

I study the message a second time, all the way through, all the way to the beeps. I listen to his voice, gruff, almost like he has to work to make it growl that deep. I listen to the way he spaces between each word, careful, like somebody might not understand his instructions, "I ... cannot ... take ... your ... call," and I wonder where he was sitting when he put that message on the machine, or if he was sitting at all. If maybe he was listening to music and turned it off for just a second. And if he was listening to music, I wonder what kind. I wonder if Leonard has ever heard his message before, and if he sounds gruff to *himself.*

A kitten chases a mouse across the kitchen floor, a little round baby mouse like you only see in picture books because they grow too fast to look that way for more than one day of their lives. A kitten chases him to the oven, where he gets away, the kitten batting at the floor where he disappeared.

I tie back my hair and walk around prissy for a while. I sit on the porch in fancy clothes and suck the dirt from beneath my fingernails until they look decent. I rest there in my swing, in the breeze, dressed up and feeling sleepy.

Then I see the flower truck driving in the gate, and I dart inside. I hadn't remembered any funeral, hadn't even heard of any deaths. And it isn't a holiday. Must be a birth or death anniversary, I think.

But the girl from the flower shop doesn't drive on up the hill to deliver her arrangement. She comes to my door, and I don't have time to change clothes before she sees me.

I go to the door and sign for the basket of tiny yellow roses like I knew they were coming all along. Though the flower girl has seen me a thousand times dressed in my work clothes, I act like a sequined gown is just the thing to wear. I act so normal in the sequined gown that I'm sure when she leaves, she wishes she had one. She climbs in her van and looks back, puzzled. I wave.

And when she is gone, I inspect the arrangement. Bud roses in greenery, little yellow heads poking up like small birds in a big nest. There's a card with my name on it, too—"Finch Nobles"—and beneath that the words "Nobles Hill," which is what everybody calls the cemetery, since it never got named proper. On the inside, the card is signed by Leonard. It doesn't say anything else. Just "Leonard"—like that should be enough.

I call him up to leave a message, glad to have a reason, but this time, he picks up the phone.

"Hello?" he says.

My air catches funny in my throat, and I can't help but wonder if those cut roses would grow if I planted them. Maybe if I planted them somewhere fertile enough. I feel myself flush hot all the way through.

"Hello?" he asks again, and I quietly put my finger down on the button to end the call.

I trip over a cat on the way to my room, with the dress already half-peeled off. I change into everyday clothes and run to lock the gate. I skip supper altogether in my hurry, because I'm foolish, feeling stupid, thinking about movies and calling a man, when I've never wanted one in my life and have got no use for one now.

I pick up the arrangement and carry it under my arm up the hill and over to the weeping willow tree. I sit the roses on Lucy's grave and wait for darkness.

HAZING MY EYES, thinning to the Dead, I watch as Lucy sniffs the buds, examining them so close, you'd think she was looking for fingerprints. "They're beautiful," she says.

"I thought you'd like them," I answer, but my voice is wrong, a lemon on a peach tree. My voice betrays me somehow.

"Where'd you get them?"

"The store," I lie. I should know better than to lie, but the words are out of my mouth before my head can catch up.

"*He* gave them to you, didn't he?" Lucy says. "Why are you lying to me?" and as she speaks, her voice ebbs, and then I lose her completely. She withdraws. She closes me out, going down lower, where I can't get. She leaves me on the ground in my clunky body.

For a while, I hold my hands on the grass and pretend that she's just on the other side, her hands held up, touching mine, mirroring mine. I pretend that death is as manageable as a wall made of ice, that we're so close, we could almost touch, that we could melt through if we held our hands there long enough.

But she's not reaching back.

"You can't *touch* me," I say. "That's the only thing wrong. It's the *only thing* you can't do." And I cry about it for a little while, like it does a bit of good.

She isn't even there. No one is. I know.

But it takes me a long time to realize that I'm the one who has receded. It takes me a long time to make my way beyond my lie, and it's like being caught in a dream, going around and around, replaying the same scene until I get it right. For a second time, I thin to the Dead. It's later now, much later, and this is what I see: William Blott at the top of the hill, playing his horn, blowing those notes out long and mournful, enough to quake my usually steady heart. He's on his knees, his head tossed back like he's daring somebody to cut his throat, and that horn an extension of his chin, so right it's like his body, like something growing out of him.

He cuts the night with those notes, and the rest of the Dead listen to his concert. He's making that trumpet wail out high, holding the note until it robs me of my lying, human breath. Baby Marcus Livingston rests at his feet, sniffling in his sleep.

Then Lucy rises up and begins to dance, making her way closer to the place where William is playing. Her hips cut crescents until they draw moons, whole skies full of moons. She moves slowly, then quicker, without losing the rhythm, and her arms tie bows around the air.

Give it to *me*, I think. Give *me* that air.

I would take anything she gave me.

But Lucy, the dancing girl, she dances to the aching horn and furnishes William Blott's song with shape. She stomps and jerks and undulates. I try to imagine her before, when she did it for a living, dancing that way. "You took off your *clothes*?" I asked her when she was new here. "How could you *do* that?"

"It was easy," she said. "My body wasn't *me*."

"Did they touch you—those men who came to see you dance?"

"Sometimes," she said. "But they weren't touching me. It was just a job, Finch. I had a nice apartment and drove a nice car. I could sleep as late as I wanted and spend the whole afternoon shopping before I went in to work. I liked it," she promised, and laughed at me for wrinkling my brow. "It was just a job."

A job that she ran to when she ran away from here. She ran away from her mama, who made her practice baton twirling every day, who signed her up for every pageant for a hundred miles around and used the money she won to register for the next pageant with a bigger award.

She ran away from her daddy, who drank too much, who made her sit on his lap wearing just her little banner and her crown while he watched NASCAR races on TV.

"You didn't have on *nothing* else?"

"Well, I had on my panties," she said. "But do you know how long a NASCAR race lasts? I had to sit that way for hours."

"What about your mama?" I asked. "Didn't your mama think that was strange?"

"No. Mama said he just wanted to hold a beauty queen, and that it should make me feel good. And then she cried because she had wrinkles and a fat ass and because he never wanted to hold her anymore."

"It must have bothered you pretty bad to run away."

"Well, I didn't run away till I was eighteen," she said. "But it did bother me. It made me feel like the worst person in the world. 'Cause I always thought there was something kind of funny about it. And if Mama and Daddy both thought it was normal, then I must have a sick mind."

"That's not logical," I told her.

"Sure it is," she answered. "You just don't like the way my heart was taught to think."

And now William Blott has called out to Lucy, and she's dancing with him, not with me. I want to holler, "Remember the scars. Ask William Blott if he has any scars." But it's too late. His horn has cast a spell. And he probably has scars anyway. He probably got run over by a lawn mower when he was a boy.

His cheeks explode the air, and that music whines on and

on in the night, and Lucy gets lost in the wave of it, or maybe the depth. She crosses her arms and clasps her hands to the hem of her tight T-shirt, lifting it to the sky and tossing it aside.

And there it is. Her bouncing chest, with the words FUCK ME etched into her skin, FUC over one nipple, KME over the other. The scars are thick cords, each letter a hundred slits, and I imagine all the blood she must have lost, how each slit must have laughed and spit and bubbled.

"I'd already been cutting myself before that happened," she told me years back. "I'd been cutting myself since before I ran away."

"Why?"

"Because," she said. "Just because."

"Dumb reason," I told her.

"It was this part of my body that nobody'd seen," she explained. "I'd do it before parades, and it made it okay somehow. I'd be riding on the back of somebody's Corvette, waving at the crowds, but underneath my dress, I had a secret. Didn't you ever see me in the Christmas parades?"

"No," I told her. And I studied her to see if she was telling the truth. "You scarred yourself on purpose?" After all my years of olive oil and peanut oil and almond oil and pig fat, I didn't know what to think.

"I just thought my body should reflect my life," she said.

And that made some sense to me.

But not FUC KME over her ninnies. That didn't make a bit of sense. That never made sense. "Were you out of your mind?" I asked her.

"No, it wasn't that," she said. "Blaine did the letters one at a time, and God, you wouldn't believe how he'd treat me afterward. I mean, he brought me flowers and rented me movies and rubbed my feet. He even cooked me dinner and fed it to me. He was *so good* to me while I was healing."

"Hmmm," I said, not saying what I was thinking.

"He didn't want me dancing. He told me I'd never have to dance again for money."

"Sounds like a real prince," I snarled.

But she was whimsical back then, and busy hiding, still protecting him, still finding ways to blame herself for every bad thing that ever happened. She talked about Blaine like he was some promised messiah. "He thought blood was so amazing. Not violence or anything like that. Just blood, and the way it moved. He'd do it in the bathtub, with me laying back with my head beneath the faucet. Without water—'cause he wanted to see the blood against the white porcelain. And I'd be sort of dizzy and usually stoned, and the blood would run off and drip down, and he'd say, 'Damn, baby, look at *all that blood*.' But I'd be so woozy by then that it'd just look like a cherry Life Saver, gathered around the drain that way."

"Blaine's gonna have some paying to do when he gets here," I told her. And already I wanted to search him down and kick his ass, because I was still alive and I could.

"He didn't hurt me," Lucy swore. "Not any more than I wanted him to."

"You trying to tell me those cuts didn't hurt you?"

"Not so much," Lucy said. "We had a pact. He'd quit anytime I said so."

"Whose idea was it?"

"His," she admitted. "But I agreed to it. He was just trying to keep me from dancing. He said he wanted me all for himself."

That was in the beginning, when she was still holding her stories in a balled-up fist, careful about how much she let out. It wasn't until later that she came to see that even if she agreed to the cutting, even if she chose the cutting, there was something terribly wrong that yielded such bad choices.

"Girl," I tried to tell her, "you were *wronged*. Even if you were wronged by yourself."

But the Mediator left her alone. The Mediator knows that all truths are partial and that what needs to come out will come out.

Like now with William Blott playing his horn. Chances are good he doesn't even know how much he's saying.

I've learned these things from watching. If it hurts you bad enough inside, the truth is the first thing to go. And so many times, the truth takes your words along with it.

But there are other ways to tell stories.

William Blott's music: *ba-ba, de-Dee, ba-Ba, ba-Ba, ba-Ba, de-Dee*—happy enough to snap your fingers to. But sure enough, it begins to limp, slipping to a lament before long, every song a pining lifting to oaks. He holds the end too long even for Lucy. She sits down naked next to Marcus and strokes his head, waiting for the next one to begin.

But it doesn't. Instead, William puts away his trumpet and settles on the ground, facedown. Then the wailing begins again, only slightly muffled by grass, and he says, "I just can't believe they'd be so petty. I just can't believe they'd be so cruel."

Lucy pulls him to her, and he sobs while the Mediator speaks.

"In the living world, there is so much fear and hatred," she says. "When we were a part of that world, we held within us that fear and that hate. When we were in the living world, we could not see what they cannot see: that the things they hate and fear are around them all the time in the things that they love."

"They were my friends," William whimpers. "They were the nicest people I'd ever met."

"And you'd have liked for them to appreciate you in death," the Mediator continues. "There were plenty of things about you to appreciate, William Blott."

"But now they hate me and I can't do anything about it."

"Knots untangle themselves," the Mediator tells him while Lucy holds him close.

Baby Marcus, who has not been outcried in years, will not be outdone. His crying is salt in a wound.

But as bad as it is to admit, I envy William Blott, rejected by everybody he knew from the living world, with all his valuables reduced to ash. I envy him for being in Lucy's arms, where I cannot go.

The knots. The tangled webs. Lucy Armageddon, who wore tap shoes and tiaras, who cropped her curls and grew them back in dreads, who let a boy carve her like a tree trunk, who danced in titty bars and drove fast cars, Lucy who said that she didn't mind the blood, who ate cotton candy for breakfast and peed on the side of the road instead of waiting for a rest stop, she found herself alone one day, in a big city, with no money and no plans.

She stood before the mirror and saw FUCK ME scrawled on her chest in the handwriting of a man who'd moved to Vegas without her. She went to her old job, and it was under new management. The owner didn't need "no scarred-up, used-up bitch" dancing on his stage, but he gave her fifty bucks for a blow job. He hooked her up with a colleague who gave her three hundred for a whole evening.

She used the money to buy the gun. Then she drove to the beach in the car that was about to be repossessed, and she kept the top down all the way and let the wind blow in her face.

She sat at the edge of the water, wearing a crown of seaweed. She danced in the waves and wailed until the surfers left. She jumped waves until her skin blistered, the tide came in, and the crowds went home. And then Lucy Armageddon wrapped herself in a fishing net. She crouched between two dunes, put the gun in her mouth, and came to me.

"Put her here," I said, because she was nobody special. Because I was sick of hearing about "that pretty little girl found dead." I knew the community wouldn't have cared so much if she'd been an ugly little girl. I staked her off a lopsided plot without shade. She was nobody I knew, and I was only getting partial payment anyway.

But I planted wildflowers on her grave out of sympathy for her mother. Her mother was taking it hard, I heard. And I am generally only sour for short periods of time.

The community rallied around Lois Armour, with her only daughter, who'd been missing for years, returned in a body bag, with her husband cuddling a bottle instead of his wife and not coming home for days or weeks at a time. People took the "murder" of "Lucille Armour" as an example of the price of youthful rebellion. "She wouldn't have never been killed by them city niggers if she'd just stayed home," Lois was fond of saying.

I heard the rumors on the street corners. After people stopped talking about her beauty, they started talking about how she died. People said she'd been stabbed, chopped, cut to shreds. People said it was a sex crime, that she had marks on her body to prove it. People said all kinds of things, wanting to believe that anybody who left behind their mother and father and church would surely have to pay with their lives. Especially beautiful people who thought they were too special to live out in the country. They wanted to think that Lucy was paying for something she'd done.

But Lucy wanted to die. She told me. "If you'd shit the bed as bad as I had, you wouldn't want to sleep in it, either," she said.

Her back was still burned from the sun, and the skin peeled away in huge strips, like wallpaper. I sat behind her and tried to pull the skin free, but whenever I'd reach for her back, I'd grab my own fingers. There was nothing in between.

I thought maybe if I touched her lightly enough, maybe if I touched her with just my mouth—and I closed my eyes and leaned to where I thought her back should be, tugging her skin between my teeth.

I thought I had some of her at first. It tasted like bits of Bible in my mouth. But later when I told the Mediator, she said it was just leftovers from my supper, a bit of pear skin, nothing more. She said there was no way I could touch Lucy, any more than I could touch Papa or Ma.

When the autopsy results came in the mail, Lois Armour had to be taken to a hospital. She fell to the floor in hysteria and lost her mind so completely that she broke wind in front of a roomful of people. Her eyes rolled back in her head and she called, "MURDER, MURDER" all down the street as the paramedics lifted her into the ambulance.

And to this day, she tries to get Lucy's story on *Unsolved Mysteries,* and she calls the FBI at least once a week for updates.

"I did it myself," Lucy insisted. "I couldn't bear it. I couldn't stand looking at those words."

"You needed a friend," I told her.

"Yeah," she agreed. "I guess that's the one thing I didn't have."

So when Lucy holds on to William Blott, who died a lovable drunk and after his death turned into a monster, I suppose Lucy knows how he feels, in a way. She is not the woman her mother grieves, any more than William Blott is the man Reba Baker hates. The idea of the person and the heart of the person—those are wholly different landscapes.

But still, it is hard to be here, on the outside, hearing the stories, hearing the horn, unable to touch them and forcing every connection. I leave the yellow flowers, all except for one.

I'm not what you think, I want to shout. I'm not *that*.

But what I say is different. What I say is whispered. "Remember the scars." And heard by nobody at all.

T HE OUTSIDE OF my house is covered with ivy. In winter, the vines mimic my skin: pale brown, intricate, netted. Fingers inching everywhere. I like it because it's ivy and because I never have to paint.

In summer, when the leaves bloom, my house becomes a living thing. The runners reach into the windows, and if I don't pay attention, I find ivy dipping into the kitchen sink or sneaking across my bookcase. I have to clip the spaces around windows before the vines grow too thick.

The cats can race right up the walls. I hear them some nights crossing over my head, their paws scratching at shingles. And if a snake or two takes cover here, what business is it of mine?

The Vegetable Man keeps telling me that the vines will hug the walls too tight and one day destroy them. He says, "You better chop them vines down 'fore it gets any worse. You'll need a crowbar just to pull off what's growed this year."

I ask him how long it will take before my house is consumed, but he doesn't know. I just let it grow. I'm only partly at home here, and I've been here forever. Why should I uproot something else?

Even when I pull back the running vines that have crept into the windows, they leave little bits of twine behind, bits of what they could be. The sound of that tearing reminds me of being scraped away.

On the porch, I lift the tentacles of my hanging Pathos plant and drape them around the frame of the roof, outlining the beams in green. When I water the plant, the moisture travels along the stem and forms a single drop at the tip of the last leaf on every tentacle. I sit in the swing and watch them hold on like a secret before quietly dropping.

One day when everything is planted, I'm going to name this cemetery Eden and lock the gate for good.

Y OU KNOW," I tell baby Marcus, "I don't understand why you cry so hard. Seems to me like you ought to save up that crying for times when you're with people you don't like."

"What makes you think he likes you?" Lucy asks. She's still pissy over the Leonard flowers. Or maybe her muscles are sore from all that dancing. Or maybe she just doesn't want to be babysitting again, but William Blott is raging, and Marcus is too young to hear the kind of language he's using.

In any case, Lucy's sour, so I ignore her. Maybe she just slept too late and woke up wrong, but I've been awake forever. I've picked up trash and scrubbed the mold off three green stones. I'm doing my best and feeling fine, and no little leftover homecoming queen is going to ruin my day. I walk a few steps ahead and lead them through the trail down to the river.

"You know," I tell Marcus, "there are a lot of advantages to learning to talk. For one thing, you could tell your story and get it over with. But besides that, you could grow up a little bit. The kids have a hell of a time. Shoot, if you were walking and talking on your own, you could go out with them at night and pull pranks. You could take the change the preacher leaves on his nightstand and arrange it along the tops of his picture frames—little dimes and nickels standing on their sides. Or you could turn his pictures upside down. Don't that sound like fun to you?"

"Are you trying to talk his ear off, or what?" Lucy asks.

"Do you hear him crying?" I retort, and as soon as I say it, I see his face crumpling, his lip pouting ugly, and I realize I'll have to watch my tone. But I don't give him time for the tears. "You got a big old lip there, boy," I tell him. "Looks like you got stung by a bee. You ever been stung by a bee?" He stares at me, puzzled, threatening to cry. It's a wonder his lungs haven't worn away.

"One time I got stung by a bee right on my lip, 'cause I was eating clover by the handfuls. I was little like you—a little bigger, I guess—and a bee stung me right on my bottom lip, and it swoll up just like yours. Felt like that bee'd somehow got inside my lip and was buzzing around in there, humming fat. Did a bee get your lip? Is that why you're pouting?"

Lucy begins to relax as I put on a show for Marcus, poking out my own lip. I'm walking backward, too, turned around to address him but still moving toward the river, and when I stumble over a root and almost trip, he laughs.

"The boy laughed!" I call out loud. "Did you hear that, Lucy? The boy laughed!"

And Lucy laughs, and baby Marcus laughs harder. We all laugh to hear him tickled. It's a new sound, like the first drips of a thaw coming to end a silent freeze. His laugh is the sound of hope, and it surprises me and Lucy—and maybe even Marcus himself.

But I don't trust it. I don't give him time to remember what it is that plagues him so.

"You ever eat clovers?" I ask. "Lord, they're good. Medicinal, too. If you have indigestion, eat a clover—but watch out for bees."

"He doesn't understand what medicinal means," Lucy notes. "He's a baby. Besides, he's dead. How's he gonna get indigestion?" We've reached the edge of the water, and I find my green wooden boat that I've chained to an oak.

There's a water moccasin curled up next to the cooler, beneath the seat. Nothing a snake likes more than a boat left in shade.

"Hold up," I say. "Gotta get rid of this snake," and I look around for a stick or boat paddle.

But Lucy puts Marcus in the boat, and he chases the snake away, right over the side and into the water.

"I forget you don't have to worry about things," I joke. "Maybe you can come over later and talk some of those black widows living in my woodpile into moving to Kalamazoo."

Marcus giggles.

"You like that word?" Lucy asks. "You like Kalamazoo?"

"Zoo," he says, and me and Lucy nearly choke.

"Damn," I say, and Lucy stares at him.

When we're on the water, and we're paddling along easy beneath big limbs dripping with moss and shadow, Lucy declares that we should play River King and Marcus can be the king. She makes him a crown from fishing lures, and then she belts out an opera about how Marcus is the mighty commander of the legions. Her voice is pretty enough, but just so loud. Marcus wrinkles his forehead and looks at me.

"Lucy," I say. "You're scaring the child."

"He likes my singing. Don't you like my singing?"

But Marcus just grunts.

"Okay," I say. "Let's make this an educational trip. Facts and distinctions. We've got to teach you the facts and distinctions. Where to start?"

Marcus stares at me, all serious, like a little scholar, or maybe like he thinks I've lost my mind. He's reverted back to his pout, though. I'm not sure if he's sad or if his mouth has grown that way.

"Bees," I say. "Now, bees are round, but hornets are wiry. And dirt dobbers, in their mud caves, are black and do not sting."

"Bees live in hives, but hornets live in triangle nests. And yellow jackets live in holes in the ground," Lucy tells him.

"Like you," I say. "You're like a yellow jacket."

He looks at us, back and forth, quiet for a change and taking it all in.

"Bees make honey, and dirt dobbers make tunnels. But yellow jackets just make noise."

And we all get silly, and I splash at the water with my paddle to wet them, and I point out a snake swimming nearby.

"Snakes," I say. "Snakes travel just as fast in the river as they do on the land. But they can't bite you as easy, 'cause when they open their mouths, they fill up with water and start to sink. When you're fishing, you have to look up in the trees to make sure a snake's not about to drop in your boat."

And we all look up, but there's no snake.

"A dying snake will tie itself in a knot," Lucy tells him.

"Is that the truth?" I ask her.

"I think so," she says. "If you hit one on the highway, it'll make a ball and bounce right down the road."

"Huh," I say. "I've hit a snake before and it just lay flat."

But Marcus isn't listening to us anyway. He's pointing to another little head stuck up in the water, like the snake I'd pointed out, but on the other side of the boat.

"That one's not a snake," I tell him. "That's a turtle. And they're hard to tell apart when they're swimming, but if you'll look at the way they move, if you'll look really good, you'll see that snakes do more of a wiggle. They skim over water, while turtles are bobbers. But turtles are much faster in the water than they are on land."

We look at some turtles sitting on a log, sunning, and a big one plops off for us, splashing fine. Then Marcus cocks his head and listens, and I can only wonder which sound has caught his ear. He begins imitating toads, calling back to them so clearly that there could be a toad in the boat.

"Sounds," I say. "He likes sounds."

Lucy takes the paddle and slaps it on the water. "This is what it sounds like to spank, and the sound that comes right after is the sound of a splash."

"This is what it sounds like to breathe," I tell him, and Lucy leans his ear up to my chest. I cannot feel him, but I can see the recognition in his eyes. I breathe deep and let him hear that air moving in and out.

"And this is what it sounds like to wait," Lucy says, and puts his ear next to her chest.

"This is what it sounds like to burn," I say, and I sizzle for him, *szzzz*.

"This is what it sounds like to blow up," Lucy says, and goes *k-Pwoooooww*.

Marcus rasps from deep in his throat, "Ahhow, ahhow."

"That's the sound of cancer of the larynx," I laugh. "Or emphysema."

Marcus keeps doing it, his face distorting so much, he begins to purple.

"Or the sound of gasping," Lucy says. "Is he strangling on something?"

But we don't get much further than that, because Leonard shows up, pushing his way between branches and clodding down to the bank, calling out, "Finch? Finch!"

"Shit," Lucy says, and I notice that Marcus has begun to cry, though I'm not sure exactly when he started. I'm glad that he's at least found air again. His coloring's coming back— though it was never all that good.

"I'll ignore him," I tell Lucy. "I'd rather be with you."

"Like it's that easy," she answers. "The bastard. And Marcus was doing so well."

And I paddle the boat around a bend, hoping that Leonard can't see.

"Finch!" he hollers out over the water. "Who're you talking to? Come on to shore. I gotta speak with you about this letter you sent Lois Armour."

"That wasn't me," I claim. "It was my secretary."

"What *letter*?" Lucy asks.

"I'm sorry, but I've got no choice," Leonard shouts. "Come on, now."

"What letter?" Lucy asks again. And I can't keep up with both worlds at the same time. They're speaking to me, but saying different things, and it's too much. Just seeing both worlds crosses my eyes, back and forth. It spins in my head, and I begin to understand how difficult it is when realities overlap. It makes sense why truths exclude each other.

I only have one mouth.

"I forgot to tell you," I say to Lucy. "I invited your mother to visit like you asked."

"I'm coming," I call to Leonard, who has already waded out to the top of his boots.

"Go see what he wants," Lucy says. "We'll be watching." And then she dives overboard, with the screaming Marcus beneath her arm. They don't even splash when they enter the water, but I can still hear Marcus, muted and miserable beneath me.

I paddle my way back toward Leonard but stop short of shore. He wades out midway to his knees and says, "Come on in. Toss me the rope."

But I say, "No. I haven't even caught a mess for supper. Whatcha want?"

"I wanna talk to you," he says.

"Thank you for the flowers," I tell him, and as I say it, I feel a thump directly beneath my boat, as if an alligator's smacked the underside with its tail. But there's no real reason for an alligator to care one way or another about the flowers Leonard sent.

"You're welcome," he says. "I'm glad you liked them. Throw me your rope."

"No," I say. "I don't believe I want to." And without even paddling, I feel my boat backing up. And I know it's Lucy and Marcus moving me out to the center of the river.

"Then I'll have to come get you," Leonard says, and he goes under, swimming beneath dark water. Water ripples all around.

I can hear Marcus screaming and Lucy cussing, distantly, and I know that all three of them are down there together.

But the closer Leonard gets to me, the farther away Marcus swims. And Lucy has to chase him, of course. She'd have a hard time explaining it to the Mediator if Marcus got lost.

I see Lucy and the screaming baby surfacing and making their way to the bank, dripping and scowling, just as Leonard comes up beside the boat.

He nearly tips me over climbing in. I have to reach my hand out to tug him and then lean backward, pulling him toward me.

"Now come on, Finch," he says, dripping everywhere, water pouring in streams behind his ears. "Truth is, I gotta take you to jail. You violated the terms of your restraining order. Either give me the paddle or take this craft to shore. You're under arrest."

"I ain't going to jail," I tell him. "I'm going fishing. I happen to have an extra pole, and you're welcome to join me."

Leonard's breathing hard. He wipes the water from beneath his chins. He's had a new haircut, a buzz, and with his hair so short, it doesn't look as dark. He's out of shape, and drenched and heavy. The front end of the boat's sunk so much lower that I'm lifted up like a queen in the back, like somebody able to walk on water.

"Please don't make me charge you with resisting arrest."

"I'm not *making you* charge me with anything," I say.

"Why'd you send that letter?"

"I sent one to everybody with a relative buried here. Didn't you get the one I sent on your brother Marcus's behalf?" And I have to stifle the screaming I hear from the bank. I pick up a pole and adjust the hook and cork.

"Probably went to Daddy," Leonard answers. "I don't know nothing about it."

"I see," I tell him, and bait his line, then hand the pole to him. "You done much fishing?"

"No," he tells me. "Finch—"

"You mean your daddy never took you fishing?"

"My daddy never took me nowhere, and you know it. He didn't want to be seen with me 'cause I was a *crybaby*."

I like his passion, so I leave him alone.

"You *know* all that. Why're you trying to rub it in?" he asks.

"I ain't rubbing nothing in," I tell him. "I just figured I ought to know how much fishing experience you've had. I didn't expect to get a confession about your relationship with your daddy. You volunteered all that."

"Oh," he says.

"See here," I tell him. "Here's all you got to know." And in my mind, I think of him a little bit the way I think about baby Marcus. He's not so awful—just annoying. He needs some teaching. That's all.

"Here's your first lesson in fishing," I tell him. "Fish won't bite when the moon's full. They'll just nibble at the bait, but they won't pull the cork under. That's okay, though. We're under a new moon, so we should be able to catch a mess. Throw your line right there in that grass bed."

"Finch," he tries to interrupt . . .

But I don't let him. "That's good. Make sure the line went down. Yeah. Now, today we're fishing for brim. Brim bite the heads off crickets first. And they won't bite at a cricket after the head is gone. You can forget it if the head's gone."

And then the cork goes under and the line starts singing, and I clap my hands for Leonard and tell him to pull it in.

But he's too slow. He loses the fish, and, of course, it got his bait—the head anyway. "Give it here," I tell him, and I stick another cricket on his hook. "Try it again."

"Finch, that piece of paper you signed was like a contract," Leonard tries to explain. I reckon he thinks I'm simple. "We had faith in you to uphold your end of the deal, and you didn't." He speaks to me, but he stares at the orange cork, bobbing there at the end of the line.

He gets another bite, and loses the fish again.

"Hand me the hook," I say, pretending to be put out.

"I can bait my own hook," he says. And he does. It takes him a while and he loses a cricket, but he does manage to get one on.

But by the time he's done it, I've paddled us down beyond the grass bed, to a place with a hollowed-out tree and lots of stumps.

"Throw it up near that tree," I tell him. "Not too high, now. There's a nest of hornets in that limb."

He looks up at the buzzing hornets and cuts his eyes. "Are you trying to kill me? What'd you move me for? I had a fish *waiting* for me back there."

"No, you didn't," I tell him. "You ran him off, spanking at the water and jerking your pole like you did. And you ran off all his brothers and sisters, too. Brim are nervous, scared fish. When you hook one, you have to pull it around to the other side of the boat to keep from scaring the other ones. You have to make it look like the caught fish is just swimming away. It's kind of like lying," I tell him. "You tell a lie, you got to pull it off for the entire crowd. You any good at lying?"

"Not as good as you are," he says.

"I'm a lot of things, but I ain't a liar," I tell him. "And I didn't never put my name on that piece of paper y'all gave me to sign."

But he doesn't believe me. He says he saw that signed piece of paper—like signing and signing *my name* are the same thing.

Between the two of us, we catch a mess of fish pretty quick. Not counting the ones we throw back, we take home eight.

Except we don't really take them home. We put them in my cooler and stick the cooler in Leonard's backseat. On the way to the police station, he stops for a bag of ice to keep them from rotting, and he gets us both a Coca-Cola. I tap the bag on the ground a couple of times to break up the large chunks and then dump the ice over the still-floundering fish.

When I get back in the car, Leonard reads me my rights and offers me some peanuts.

I T'S LATE IN the afternoon by the time we get to the police station, and then there are complications. As soon as I arrive, Leonard gets summoned outside, and I can't see him because the door is made of smoky glass. Problem number two: I don't have a lawyer. The soft-faced boy who's doing all the paperwork says I'm going to need one.

"Get Leonard for me," I tell him.

"Leonard ain't no lawyer, and he's got another assignment anyway," the young man says. "There's a car wreck over on Highway Nine."

"I ain't got no lawyer," I tell him. "And I don't believe you about that wreck, either. Leonard didn't say he was going to any wreck."

"It just happened, Miss Nobles. He's really gone. Now look here. This is a list of lawyers with their phone numbers. You need to just pick one and call."

"I don't want to pay for no lawyer," I tell him. "I ain't done nothing wrong."

"You harassed Ms. Lois Armour," he tells me. He's too young to listen. He ought not be allowed to carry a gun.

"I'll represent myself," I tell him. "You show me the evidence."

"We have your signature," he reminds me. He was the boy that got my signature in the first place.

"Show me," I say.

But the records office is already closed. Closed until eight o'clock tomorrow morning.

"You mean I'm stuck here all night?"

"Yep," he answers. "You were stuck here all night anyway."

"Get me the judge," I tell him. "I wanna talk to the judge."

"Do you see any judge here?" he asks. "If you want counsel, call a lawyer."

"Get Leonard," I say. "He'll post my bond."

"Lady, you don't know much about the law, do you? We got rules here. Rules we follow. Leonard can't bail you out because your bail ain't been set," the boy tells me. "The arresting officer ain't allowed to post bond anyway—especially not when the officer is a single man and the criminal is a pretty lady," and he darts his eyes away from me when he says that—'cause he knows I'm a far stretch from pretty. "And besides that, he's at the wreck. You deaf or something?"

"What kind of police department are you running?" I ask him.

"A damned good one," he tells me, puffing his chest like a rooster.

"I'd like to see your handbook of the law," I say, but he just laughs.

He takes my picture and rolls my fingers over a piece of cardboard, but he doesn't put me in special clothes or anything fancy. He puts me in a big cell all by myself, with my pick of cots.

"You don't have no other prisoners?"

"No other women," he tells me. "We got a man on the other side."

My cell is right beside the desk where I checked in. "It'll give you something to look at," the boy-faced officer says.

"What if I have to use the bathroom?"

"Pull the curtain."

So I sit in my cell, twiddling my thumbs and picking at a mole on my wrist. The officer calls out to me periodically, "You okay in there, Miss Nobles?"

"Fine," I say. "Thank you for caring."

"You get ready to confess, you just let me know."

"Okay," I say. "But don't get your hopes up."

"You get ready to call a lawyer, just say the word. You get a free phone call, you know."

"Alrighty." I sit in there for a long time, feeling kind of bad because I didn't feed the cats. I try to remember whether or not they had any food left in their bowls from yesterday, but I doubt it. Woe to the birds and mice, to the bugs that live in the ivy.

Then a different police officer brings me some supper, and it's not as bad as you might think. He brings me candied yams and some rice with gravy and a piece of meat—I can't tell what kind—and a cup of watery tea. And I eat it, 'cause all I've had is a pack of Nabs and a handful of peanuts since breakfast.

My hands still smell like fish, and my fingers stick a little when I press them together. It's hot in the jail, and that does nothing for the smell. The smell of food and armpit hovers in the air, and I think they ought to get an exhaust fan to make it more pleasant.

Then Leonard comes back, and he brings me a cheeseburger and some french fries. I'm kind of glad to see him, but also miffed that he left me that way, wreck or no wreck.

"I was gonna try to fry up them fish," he says. "But the

accident took me too long. I didn't want you to get stuck eating mystery meat." He pulls up a chair and sits backward in it, leaning his fat belly against the backing, and he eats his supper with me, chewing and talking at the same time. "Phillips says you don't want a lawyer. I got to advise you to get one, Finch. A judge ain't gonna be kind to you. He's gonna feel real sorry for Lois Armour."

"Who would you recommend?" I ask.

"T. J. Wilson?" he suggests.

"I don't know of him," I say. "I'd rather have somebody I know of."

"Wilson's good," he tells me.

"Mmmm, I don't know. I just like the idea of having a lawyer from my own community."

"Ain't no lawyers in our community."

"There's one," I say.

Leonard thinks for a second, then jumps up and moves his face right to the bars, leaning in a little, so that his nose actually goes through, so he's just inches from my face. "No," he says, and I can see a bit of lettuce wedged between his front two teeth. "Father's in retirement. And besides that, damn it, he hardly practiced law at all. Once he became an elected official, he only tried four or five cases. He hasn't been in a courtroom in twenty years."

"I think that's who I want," I tell him. "Can you get me his number?"

"He might not even be licensed anymore. He's *not well,* Finch," Leonard insists.

He clings to the bars, and I study his fingers, stained yellow with mustard.

"Mother just came home from the hospital, and Father's got her to take care of. He's an *old man*. He's half-senile already," he pleads. Then adds, "What have I done to you, damn it?"

"You got me arrested. That's one thing," I say. "And then—"

"Oh no," he interrupts. "You did that to yourself. I've been as kind to you as I can be." He's red-faced and puffing, with sweat stains arcing halfway down his shirt. "Business is business, and arresting you was my business. Letting you have your afternoon fishing and bringing you something good to eat so you wouldn't have to eat the jailhouse food, that was something *else*," and he throws me an apple pie, still warm in its red container, and walks away. "Phillips, get her the telephone," he says, and he slams the door.

Phillips looks at me, and I look at Phillips.

"I musta said the wrong thing," I tell him.

"I reckon you did," he answers. "You want the phone?"

"Not yet," I say. "I was half-teasing—about calling his father, I mean."

"Leonard ain't the teasing kind," Phillips tells me. "He walks around here half the time like he's lost his best friend. Yeah, Leonard wears his britches too tight for sure."

"Well," I answer, "he's had a hard row to hoe. Even when we were little, his father didn't think much of him."

"You and Leonard the same age?" he asks me, like he can't believe it. And I know it's 'cause I look so much older, with my wadded-up face.

"Yeah."

"Say then, maybe you can tell me what happened to Leonard when he was seven years old."

"What are you talking about?"

"I was weeding through everybody's health files the other day, updating them because we're about to have an inspection, and a letter fell out of Leonard's folder. It was a permission slip for him to serve as an officer of the law—because he'd had some sort of blot on his record as a young child. The letter referred to extenuating circumstances and childhood traumas—I don't know. Whatever it was happened when he was seven. But he had to get special approval to become a policeman."

"Well, he got the approval, obviously, so I reckon it ain't no business of yours or mine, neither one," I tell Phillips. 'Cause there's no reason for some upstart policeman with little willowy sideburns to be tearing a fellow like Leonard down.

"I just wondered," he says, and he turns on the television, but I can't see it.

After a while, it starts to thunder a little and Phillips muses and turns the TV off. "I love a storm," he says—to me, I guess, since no one else is around.

"Me, too," I tell him.

"It's supposed to rain," he says. "They're calling for rain tonight."

I sit in my cell until everything's quiet. As time goes on, Phillips dozes at his desk. Suddenly, I hear it loud on the roof, rain falling fast, and Phillips sighs in his dreams at the sound of it. And as he sleeps, the Poet and Papa come in for a visit, leaking into my cell in raindrops, then taking their regular shapes.

"Hey, sugar," Papa says. "You all right?"

"Yes, sir," I whisper. "I'm fine. What're you doing here? *How* are you here?"

The Dead don't often stray off in the nights—particularly

not when the weather's bad. They like to sleep like everybody else, and when they get wet, the grave seems even colder.

But even more, the police station is ten miles away, and there are other cemeteries in between. So Papa and the Poet are out of their jurisdiction. They have no real reason to be here.

"An act of self-defense," the Poet proclaims. "Marcus's voice has found a new volume. I try to tell him that volume's a privilege, not a right, but he doesn't seem to understand . . ."

"A lot's happened since you've been gone," Papa says. "The Mediator sent me here to warn you. *He* just tagged along."

"I was getting a headache," the Poet explains. "Don't worry, Finch. If they don't let you out before long, we'll rig up a tornado to take the top off the building. It'll fly like a kite, and you can be the tail, and you can let go anywhere you like."

"How's William Blott?" I ask.

"Just terrible," Papa says. "Something's happened. I wanted you to know, in case you got out. Some of those boys came in under the fence and spray-painted bad words on William's stone."

"What words?"

"*Faggot,*" the Poet says deadpan. "*Queer. Cocksucker, butt-fucker, ass-pirate—*"

"She gets the picture," Papa says.

"Ass-pirate!" I chuckle. "That's pretty good!"

"They didn't make it up." The Poet sniffs. "It's a British term."

"I guess William was pretty upset about it," I say.

"Yeah," Papa replies. "Especially when we found out that all those boys went to Glory Road afterward. They were boys from the church. And Reba made them all ham biscuits, served 'em supper for free!"

"How'd you find out?"

"Oh, I was roaming about," the Poet admits. "I was on the roof of the store when it happened, changing the course of this little storm we located over the Atlantic. I don't want the whole place destroyed or anything, but if Marcus doesn't quit crying . . ." and he drifts off.

"We've called in a big, *big* storm," Papa tells me. "But this here piddly cloud ain't it. The Dead in these parts ain't even *involved* in our storm."

"Oh no," the Poet allows. "Our storm's going to make this one look like a measly pissing."

"Everybody's ready for William to get his revenge," Papa explains. "So he can go back to being a good mother and Marcus'll shut up."

"And Lucy's upset, as well," the Poet says. "Those flowers, you know—those flowers you gave her were quicklime on her heart. And now to think that you're here—because you contacted her mother again. Aieee. By the time Leonard's squad car pulled out of the cemetery, she was tearing at her hair."

"She's bad off," Papa agrees.

"Yeah," the Poet muses. "Lucy Armageddon's kicking her feet. We're feeling it underground. She's riling up oceans. She's tapped into something big. After the storm comes here, she's going to push it all the way to Nevada, she says, to wipe out a bad memory."

"We've got to get back," Papa tells me. "I'm sorry we can't stay longer."

"That's okay," I tell them. "Thanks for coming by."

The Poet picks at a mattress, at a place where a cigarette has burned into a cot. He pulls out some fibers from inside and stuffs them in his ears. "For later," he says.

And they're gone.

I decide I may as well get some sleep, and so I choose a cot and try to settle down. But the rain continues, and the wind—and my mind picks up on the turbulence. My mind won't let me rest. It takes me a long time to fall asleep, and then suddenly I'm awakened by an old man in a baggy gray suit.

"Miss Nobles? Miss Nobles?" he calls. He lifts off a gentleman's hat, to reveal a head slick as a tick, but there are plenty of hairs left on his face. He's a bald man with a full gray mustache and eyebrows as willful as spider legs.

I stare at him, closing my eyes and reopening to distinguish which world he has come from. He's not familiar, but he's not strange.

Then Phillips runs up beside him, puzzled, and says, "I didn't realize she called you, Mr. Livingston."

"She didn't," he bellows. "I heard it from an associate, you might say. Probably an associate who's made a wrongful arrest. And what are you sleeping on the job for, anyway? I could have broken every prisoner out of this jail before you woke up. I've been watching you snore for nearly an hour!"

"Leonard called you?" I ask, my mouth thick with morning. I approach the bars and peer out.

"Indeed," the old man grunts. "He says you violated an agreement."

"Mr. Livingston," I say. "I haven't violated a *thing*." And I hold his gaze.

"Evidence?" he demands, and flattens his hand out to Phillips, though he continues looking at me.

"I'm sorry, sir," Phillips replies. "The records office doesn't open until eight."

"Open the records office or I'll have your languorous nuts with my next cup of coffee!" Mr. Livingston says. "Get me the evidence."

Phillips flushes and leaves the room.

"You have to talk hard to these fellows if you want anything done," he says, and he looks at me hard, reading my face.

"I can't believe Leonard called you."

"Why not? You requested it, didn't you?" the old man asks. "Except for public niceties, Leonard and I haven't spoken in months, so I'm certain he wouldn't have done it otherwise."

"He's a fine officer," I say.

"Leonard? Pshaw. Now, my *other* son, the one taken from me as a child, *he* was leader material, but Leonard . . . Hell, Leonard's lucky he's not a security guard by now."

Phillips returns with a copy of the paper I signed—just as Leonard arrives. The smoky door squeaks almost as fiercely as his shoes. He waves to me tersely and turns to his father.

"Father," he says, and he straightens his belt.

"Leonard," Mr. Livingston says, and nods, then turns away.

I can see that a cat's been sleeping on Leonard's pants, his backside furry and pale like the wild babies he took from my house. I'm wishing I could tell him before his father sees. On the desk, there's Scotch tape, and he could lift the fur off with that, if he knew he was furry at all.

"Here you are, sir," Phillips whispers, slipping the document into Mr. Livingston's hand.

"Let's see what we can do for you, Miss Nobles," Mr. Livingston says. Then he takes the document to Phillips's desk and sits down. He pulls out his glasses and studies it carefully. From behind my bars, I see Phillips wiping crust from his eyes, and Leonard standing with his shoulders pulled back so far his bones vee out, in military fashion The door swings open again, and this time Reba Baker strolls in, a clear plastic bonnet pulled over her head and snapped beneath her chin. She's holding and waving an envelope.

"Whatever her bail is, I've got it," she says. "I'm here to get Finch out of jail."

"This document's not even legal," Mr. Livingston spits. "Not to mention that she signed somebody else's name—Lucy Armageddon. Who's that? Maybe you'd better find out and put *her* in jail."

Phillips flushes and Leonard drops his head.

Mr. Livingston stands up and marches to where Leonard waits. "You're a *fine* officer, Leonard," Mr. Livingston says. "A *fine, fine* officer," and as he speaks, he's pounding the letter into Leonard's chest.

Meanwhile, Phillips hurriedly unlocks my cell, and I'm out of there before anybody has a chance to change his mind. I'm all the way over to the water fountain, near the exit.

"I've got *bail!*" Reba Baker declares, as though nobody heard her the first time.

I look over at Leonard, who is red-faced and sinking beneath his father's wrath, and I hate him for being such a wimp about it. But I come to his defense just the same.

"Leonard didn't draw up that document," I announce. "Phillips did. And Phillips was the one who witnessed me signing it."

Mr. Livingston gets all flustered and rubs at his nose, then returns, "But Leonard was the arresting officer."

"You're right about that. And he arrested me and hand-cuffed me and read me my rights just the way he was supposed to. But as soon as we got to the station, he got called away to an accident on Highway Nine," I insist. "Phillips is the one who fingerprinted me and kept me here all night long, even though I asked to see the evidence. And isn't he supposed to find me a free lawyer if I tell him I can't afford one?"

Phillips shrinks off into the corner, and Mr. Livingston's pale eyes follow him there.

"Boy, we gotta talk," Mr. Livingston says, and heads his way.

"Excuse me," Reba Baker says, "I've got bail." She tugs at Mr. Livingston's sleeve, but he shakes her off without seeming even to notice her.

"Reba," Leonard tells her finally, "ain't no need for bail. We're no longer holding Finch. There's been a mistake."

"I don't know if you heard or not," Reba tells me, "but the adult women's Sunday school class has chosen you as our next project, Finch Nobles. We're going to see to it that your spiritual needs are met so that you won't feel the need to harass Lois Armour anymore. And if you *had* needed bail, we were ready to supply it."

"Take me home," I say to Leonard, and he grabs my elbow and leads me toward the door.

"Hold *it*," Mr. Livingston calls, and Leonard jerks to a stop. "Your mother needs to be driven to the doctor this morning," he says. "And as you can see, I'm busy talking with Phillips here about his career in law enforcement."

"What time's her appointment?" Leonard sighs.

"In half an hour," Mr. Livingston says. "You'd better hurry."

Leonard looks at me apologetically, and then Reba Baker steps up and volunteers to drive me home. She's so cheerful, she makes me queasy. Nobody should be that cheerful early in the day—and certainly not at the jailhouse.

"My car's just out here and ready," she says.

"I'm sorry," Leonard tells me. "My mother—she's not well. You understand?"

"Yeah."

"Come on, Finch," Reba repeats, like she's under a time constraint.

"Just a second," I tell her.

I run back in to the desk, grab the Scotch tape, and pull off a couple of pieces. I offer them to Leonard, who's already on the way to his car. "A cat's been sleeping on the legs of them pants," I tell him. "On the back."

He looks at me funny, and so I slap the tape to his ass and walk on over to Reba's car. 'Cause I'm in no mood to walk the ten miles.

R EBA DOESN'T TAKE the highway. She says it's too hard on her nerves to deal with more than one lane of cars driving in the same direction. She takes Route 5, which adds some time to our trip.

The beige Plymouth hiccups around curves and over hills,

with Reba putting her foot on the gas pedal and then lifting it up, over and over.

Maybe I'm just looking hard for something to criticize. I don't know how to feel about her sudden warmth toward me.

In the cassette player, there's a tape of gospel music, bluegrass and whining, and for the first couple of miles, Reba sings along, trilling high with the tenor. I just lean my head back and study the ceiling, the way the thin beige fabric is sagging, the way Reba has secured it with thumbtacks. Then when the tape comes to an end, the cassette player spits it out, and it's quiet in the car.

"I reckon you're wondering why we chose *you*," she says.

"No," I answer. "I've got a pretty good idea."

"Oh?" she asks.

"Best I can figure, you're trying to buy your way to Heaven. So now that William Blott's dead, you gotta find somebody else to win over to Jesus. And I might not be a drunk or a bum, but I'm probably the next-best thing," I taunt. "Hell, you probably got even worse words for me than *drunk* or *bum*. I can't think offhand of anybody you'd consider a harder case."

"You're not gonna ruin my happy spirit this day, Finch, so you can just quit trying," she tells me. "*The Lord* has sent us to you."

"Is that who I should thank?" I say snidely.

"Yes it is," she replies. The woman doesn't have an ounce of wit.

We cross over a bridge and drive through a place where the trees grow tall on either side of the road. Their branches form a canopy, and on this morning, with the rain just past ended, huge drops of water fall onto the windshield each time a breeze crosses. Splat, splat, and then the windshield wipers scrape across the glass with their dulled blades.

All I can think about is getting home, getting in the house and feeding the cats, getting out to the graveyard and picking up the limbs the trees lost in the rainstorm. I'll probably have to rake, too. I'm already running late.

And then Reba gets behind a farm truck, heavy with tobacco and driving slower than I could run. We putter along, with me growing more impatient and Reba smiling at the windshield.

Finally, she begins talking with me again. "The reason we chose you, Finch, is because you are single-handedly driving Lois Armour crazy. Now, Lois has been sick for many years, but she's grown closer to God and formed close ties with the church. And even though she can't come worship with us, she's an honorary member of our Sunday school class, and we visit with her each week, and we've come to love her and want the best for her."

I listen.

"I'll tell you a fact, too. She's a marvelous woman who bears her cross without complaint. She lost her daughter and almost immediately lost her husband, who comes and goes, as you know. But now she's got God in her life, and she's doing so much better. Even as an invalid, she does volunteer work. She runs our phone tree. She organizes events for us, and I can't tell you how important she's been in all our lives. We all love Lois.

"So we decided, all of us, we decided to try to show you God's love, in the hopes that you'll stop pestering Lois Armour to death about her daughter."

"Does this mean that you'll sell my vegetables at the store?"

"No, it does *not*," Reba answers. "That ain't how God's love works."

"Will I have to be on TV?" I ask her.

"Most people like the idea of being on television," Reba defends. "And besides that, it's a good opportunity to give other congregations ideas about helping those in need."

"I'm not in need," I tell her.

"Oh, yes you are," Reba says. "You've got a problem, and it's already gotten you in jail. You've got a problem, and it's natural that you're denying it, but we want to help you, and God wants to help you."

"I appreciate the ride," I say. "And your offer to bail me out, too. But I think you better look elsewhere for your projects. Maybe Lois Armour would be a good project for you. I understand she's having some trouble admitting that her daughter committed suicide. See, if she'd just admit what everybody else knows, then I could leave her alone."

And I think for a second I might have finally shut Reba up. But I haven't. It just takes her a while to reply.

"I'll tell you a little secret," Reba mutters nasty. "Lois Armour used to *be* one of our projects. Back when she suffered the loss of her daughter and she was still overwhelmed by the things of this world, the material things that mean nothing in the next life. But God changed Lois, and he can change you. The Lord works miracles every day."

And I don't reply to that. My head hurts from a night with too little sleep, and my eyes bag from a morning with too little coffee. And I don't want to be rude to Reba or nice to Reba, either one. I just want to be done with Reba. But right before we get to my street, I hear this little click.

And then she turns left where she needs to turn right.

"Whoa," I say. "Where're you going?"

"I'm taking you out to breakfast," she tells me, but she's lying. She's got that highness in her voice that tells me so.

"Come on, now," I tell her. "Take me home."

But she doesn't. And when I try to open the door at a stop sign, I find that her Plymouth is one of those Venus-flytrap cars where you can't open the door unless you've got the driver's seat, where all the controls are situated. When I try to roll down the window, nothing happens, either.

And then I get mad, shit-ass-mad, and I start cussing her and threatening her with kidnapping charges. But Reba just smiles and snickers, without giving me the common courtesy of her eyes.

When I finally shut up, she asks, "You like the locks?"

"How'd you get security locks on this ugly junk car?"

"Had them installed just for you," she says, and I'm almost inclined to believe her.

"Where you taking me?"

"The ladies wanted to talk with you," she says. "And after we bailed you out of jail, I think talking with us is the least you can do."

"You didn't bail me out. I was out already."

"We're going to Lois Armour's house," Reba says. "We're going to help you take the first step toward healing the wounds."

Reba turns into the alley, then drives right into the backyard, where the ladies are all waiting. They're sitting in lawn chairs beneath two funeral tents—maybe because it's raining or maybe to make fun of me. They've laid out tables like it's a fancy occasion, and they've got a big banner

hanging up over some back windows that says WELCOME
FINCH NOBLES.

"Dear God," I say.

"That's right," Reba answers. "He *is* dear."

And they're all wearing pantsuits or neat dresses. They've
all got their hair teased up and sprayed tight. They're all smiling
to me and waving, like I'd be looking forward to having breakfast
with them, like I'd be grateful for all they've done.

But when I get out of the car, I'm ready for them. I've got
too much to do to have a party on a rainy morning with a bunch
of old lady hypocrites.

"I thank you for sending the bail," I announce, "but I didn't
need it. I was already out of jail when Reba arrived, and she'll
be giving you back all your money. Y'all have a good breakfast."
And I head for the gate. I'm not running, but I'm not exactly
walking, either. And I'm not looking back.

I half-expect to be tackled by the preacher's wife or a
big bull deacon, but it's Lois Armour who gets me—and with
her words, too. She says, "If you got something to say to me,
Finch, please come say it now while I got my friends around.
'Cause it tears me up when you do it and I've got no one with
me."

And I'm caught off guard—because she isn't rude at all; she
says "please." She's not what I expect, and before I even mean to,
I've turned around to look at her.

"You keep doing it to me," she says without spite. No, it's
more like resignation in her voice. "Over and over. Saying my
baby killed herself, like you even *knew* her. Like you got any idea
what happened. Why do you do that to me?"

I don't say anything. I just stand there in the drizzling rain, imagining Lucy Armageddon playing in that yard, splashing around in her pool with her friends.

"We made you some breakfast and some coffee," Lois says.

"I don't wanna be nobody's project," I tell her.

"Even so," she says. "You can still eat with us."

The other women sit quietly and agree to everything Lois says. Even Reba is quiet, though after Lois is done talking, she motions for me to come over.

I consider it for a long moment, and I consider it real good. I got no use for the church or for Reba. I'm still stewing about how they treated William Blott, and every time I look at them, I think of his face when he learned they were burning his land. I can smell the smoke in my mind.

But there's Lucy to consider, too. Maybe to get to her mama, she needs a bridge. Maybe I've been the wrong kind of bridge in the past.

So I go sit down next to Lois.

"You take milk and sugar?" she asks, and I nod.

Her hand shakes as she clenches sugar cubes between little silver tongs over my cup.

I FIND LUCY ON top of my house. She's up there, standing at the peak of my A-frame, barefoot on old shingles, and she's spinning her arms around like she's stirring the air.

"Lucy," I call to her.

But she doesn't answer. The clouds above her are dark and churning.

"Lucy," I shout, and when there's still no reply, I climb the ivy. I pull myself up with the vines, slipping and catching with just my toes. It's more like a rope than a ladder, and I'm not as adept at climbing as the cats. The ivy isn't nearly as strong as I'd thought. It keeps tearing from the walls, ripping and leaving a trail to show just where I've been. My hands strip away the spaded leaves, and by the time I reach the roof, I'm skinned and scraped and out of breath.

When I get over the edge, she looks down at me, bites her lip.

"Traitor," she accuses.

"What are you talking about?" I ask her. Though I know, of course. She's been watching.

"Bitch," she cries.

The roof slopes easy, but the shingles are slick and break off in pieces. I slip and catch myself with my hands. I approach her on hands and feet. It's steeper than it looks.

"Lucy," I say. "I've been with your mama."

"I know." She sniffs. "Did you like her?"

"Yeah, I did. I didn't choose to go over there, but I stayed of my own accord. And yeah, I liked her all right."

"Figures."

She's crying so hard that her tears fall into my hair. "Well, tell me what happened," she says. "Tell me everything."

And I have some answers for her this time.

"She was wearing navy slacks and a matching top with an anchor stitched on it in white and gold."

"Sounds tacky."

"She looked nice," I tell her. "She was wearing makeup—pink frosty lipstick and cheek stuff."

"Rouge."

"Yeah, and her hair was blond and curled—kind of fancy. It hung to her shoulders. It was sprayed."

"She dyes it," Lucy tells me, like it's some kind of crime.

"So what?" I say. "It looked pretty. I've been thinking of dying *my* hair."

"You should do it red," Lucy says. "I'll help you. Tell me more."

"She says you were never the suicide type," I continue. "Her basic argument goes like this: You were sunburned when you died. She says it doesn't make sense for a person who's thinking of killing herself to bother with tanning."

"Geez, that's not even logical," she shouts up at a cloud.

"Oh, sure it is," I answer, and then I repeat one of her own lines: "'You just don't like the way her heart was taught to think.'"

She drops her arms and stares at me.

"Come on," I say. "Let's get down."

She goes ahead of me and holds the ivy up so I won't fall. Then, when we're on the ground, Lucy leads me to the bushes that line the cemetery fence for a ways. They're pokeweed bushes, and the clusters of berries hang ripe and burgundy. She begins picking them off in whole clumps, dropping them in a bowl licked clean by cats.

"Was she crying?" Lucy asks.

"She cried a little bit," I tell her.

"When did she cry?"

"She was walking me through the house. You see, she

wanted me to get to know you," and I laugh. "She said that if I'd known you, I'd understand how you couldn't have never committed suicide."

Lucy rolls her eyes.

"So she was showing me around. I saw all your dancing pictures. You were cute," I tell her.

"A*dor*able."

"You were grinning in those pictures like you had the world in your hand."

"I didn't," Lucy whispers.

"But, baby, nobody ever does. Your mama, she showed me all your crowns. She's got 'em lined up in a doll case. She showed me your trophies and even a little porcelain doll she ordered out of a catalog—had it made from one of your pictures."

"I forgot about that," Lucy says. "And it made her cry to look at it?"

"Oh, no," I tell her. "She was happy showing you off. She said you made her proud, that you did all the things she never got to do."

"When did she cry?"

"When she talked about you running away. She said it was a wonder God let her keep you for as long as he did."

Lucy looks at me, studying me, then asks, "What'd she mean by that?"

"She said it was a wonder you were able to make your own way and live the life that you wanted to lead. Said she tried so hard to force you into being what *she* wanted you to be that it was a miracle you were able to break free and be yourself."

"*My* mama said that?"

"She did."

"You're lying," Lucy says, testing me.

"I'm a lot of things, but I ain't a liar," I answer.

"You are sometimes," she says, and she's right.

Lucy leads me to the back doorsteps, a big bowlful of berries in her arms. We sit there and she mashes the berries with her fingers, picking out the stems. Her fingers are the color of new blood.

"This is how me and Charles Belcher used to dye our hair. Berry dyes last a long time." Then she sighs. "Oh, Finch, I don't know what to think."

"I'll give you a clue," I offer. "Your mama might not have been the best mama in the world. She might've put you in hard situations that you didn't like, and she might've done you wrong in other ways. But she's human, Lucy. She's bound to make mistakes."

And Lucy begins rubbing my hair with the berry paste, and I can almost feel her, almost. The berries are in my hair, and I can reach up and redden my fingers, but I can't quite feel Lucy behind it all. Not quite.

I tell her, "You got to stop this storm. You got to make them stop it."

"I can't do that," she says.

"Tell me why."

"It's too late. And besides, I've given it all my energy already. Now it's feeding off of William and Marcus. I'm just the choreographer. That's all."

"But your mama," I say. "She's not as blind as you thought."

"She still can't admit how I died."

And I turn around sharp to address her. "You think about whether you want her to," I say. "You think about it hard. Because she *did* love you—even if she loved you wrong. And she *does* miss you. But she's a religious woman, believing all the Bible tells her. The minute she admits it's a suicide, that's the minute she has to think of you in Hell. Either that, or else her whole faith crumbles. And do you really want either one of those things for her? Especially when you ain't there to replace what you're taking?"

"I don't know," Lucy says. "Bend your head."

And she rinses the berries away with the rainwater that's collected outside my door. The concrete steps rinse to pink.

"Please stop the storm," I beg her.

"I can't," she tells me. "It's too late. Too much has happened."

"It won't hurt anybody, will it? The storm? It's just a sign, right?" "I don't know." But she won't look at me. She won't look me in the eyes.

"Don't do it," I say, and Lucy leans into me, because we cannot touch. She leans her lips into my cheek. And though I don't feel her lips, I know the kiss. I know what it means.

"Thanks for everything," she says, then adds, "I'm so sorry." And she is gone.

T HE SKY GROWS darker, but the air grows still. Still and warmer, and the rain has stopped. The air feels thick as a dead man's tongue, and I walk up the hill, my purple hair shining. I walk up the hill with a pail of soapy water and a bottle of bleach, and I intend to keep quiet and leave the Dead alone because I can feel them raging. I can feel it in the trembling ground. And their anger is bigger than anything in me. I am, after all, a part of the living world. Nothing could be more clear now.

William Blott's monument beckons like a sign: "Faggot" and so on.

I start scrubbing.

I pour on the bleach and I scrub with a brush. I scrub with all my weight behind me, scouring against insults. "You do not deserve this," I whisper as I work. "You're not a bad man, and this shouldn't have happened to you. Not everybody in the world feels this way, and even the ones who do—they can learn maybe—"

But all my cleaning is not enough. I cannot get the words to disappear. I can fade them, but there are remains, traces of hate at his grave.

"William," I say. "I'm so sorry."

And I keep right on. I work too hard to concentrate enough to haze to the Dead, and there's nothing I could do there anyway. But I can hear William Blott playing his horn again, in the distance. It mourns deep down, like a man has to do when he can't say what's wrong outright.

At some point, Reba Baker shows up. I hear the car coming way before I see it, and I'm half-hoping it's Leonard. But then it's a Plymouth—a puke-colored Plymouth with doors just Reba can lock.

She approaches the place where I'm working, and I reckon she thinks we're friends now. She must think we've become friends, because she says, "Well, my mercy, look at that hair. How'd you have time to get to a beauty shop, Finch?"

"I didn't," I tell her, though I don't stop what I'm doing. "I just used some berries out of the yard."

"A berry job. Now that's something. See here, I wanted to tell you . . . Well, why're you crying? What's the matter, honey?" she asks.

"I ain't crying," I lie. "I've got soap in my eyes."

"Let me see," and she grabs my chin and lifts it right up. Nobody has ever grabbed my chin that way—not since the scrapings. And Reba says, "No, darling, you're crying. Has this day just been too much?"

And about that time, my day is too much, and about that time, I squall wicked. "Would you look at this stone?" I wail. "Would you look at what they've done?"

"You shouldn't take that personally, honey," Reba says. "Nobody meant nothing toward *you*, so don't take it that way. This here was just done in protest of William Blott and his life-style of degradation."

I sit right down on the place I've been wiping. I plop down in the soapy water and bleach and I turn to look at Reba and I say, "How can you treat him this way?"

"What do you mean?"

"How can you get to know a person and then turn on him the way you did? Even a dog who gets the shit beat out of it don't bite the hand that feeds it—or the one that beats it—or its friends. Damn it, you know what I mean."

"He was a *queer*, Finch. God don't love a queer." And the only solace I take is in imagining Reba hatching maggots after she dies.

"I don't know if you heard or not, but he was a queer. And we were all just so hurt by it. We were so hurt that he would come into our homes and pray with us and then leave and do the things people like him do."

"That's not a good answer, Reba," I say. "That's about the worst answer I ever heard from somebody who calls herself a Christian."

She looks at me surprised.

"And that's not an excuse, neither—not for all *this* painted on his grave!"

She looks around at the words, then sees the word *butt-fucker* and points and covers her mouth.

"Now they shouldn't have written that one," she says. "That's an awful word."

"You think that's bad, the other side says '*ass*-pirate,'" I tell her.

Reba sucks in her air.

"You know why I ate breakfast with you hussies today?" I ask her, and I'm stammering and choking out the words by now, because I've gone chilly in my soul. "I stayed there because it occurred to me that I might be wrong about Lois Armour. Now, I still believe that Lucy killed herself. I know she did. But it occurred to me that maybe I was wrong to say so in front of Lois. 'Cause it ain't my business what she believes or what she does. I can't do nothing *about* what she believes or what she does. I'm just responsible for me."

"I reckon you're right," Reba says. "But that still don't give you reason to call us hussies."

"And I've been wrong to devil-hack her the way I did," I admit. "And I'm sorry about it."

"Praise the Lord for *that*," Reba whispers.

"But you see, I got a *real* problem with you treating

William Blott this way." And I'm talking so loud that the words are vibrating inside my head.

"Now, Finch, that's different," she says.

"Ain't different," I tell her. "It ain't. And it ain't your place to cast aspersion on him no matter what he was. If you meant *a thing* you said in that paper, if you meant it even for a *second* when you told that reporter that William Blott had enriched your life, then why in God's name would you turn on him after he died?"

"I can't abide a queer, Finch," Reba says, but she's breaking. She's breaking right down.

William Blott blows on his horn. He blows it like a freight train. He blows it like a storm. And he starts playing "When the Roll Is Called Up Yonder I'll Be There," and Reba turns her head toward him, like she almost hears him, and she says, "Finch, I believe the air moves different on this side of the hill. Does it sound different to you?"

"No," I tell her quietly. "It just sounds normal."

Reba cocks her head and listens good, and William Blott keeps playing, and I say, "Why *did* you take on William Blott?"

"I don't *know,*" she tells me, and from the way she says it, I believe her. "I don't know exactly. There was something about him that was so playful—like in spite of all his drinking and all his problems, he had good cheer. He didn't say much, but what he said, he said sweet."

"Yeah," I say. "He always seemed that way to me, too."

"And he could sing. Lord, he could sing so pretty. If we could've got him in the church, he'd have *made* that choir. I told him one time that he ought to come sing us a song. And he asked me what my favorite song was, and when I told him, he said he'd play it on his trumpet one day and I could sing it."

Then the horn gets louder, and William Blott plays that song for Reba, and she starts humming along, just a little.

"I'll tell you, that wind is blowing *funny* through these trees," she says. "It almost sounds like a song."

But there are nearby trees all around, and none of them are moving. The air is still, solid as a bone.

"He *did* sing pretty," Reba tells me. "He could raise the goose pimples on my arms. Just thinking about it gives me goose pimples," she says. "See?" And she shows me. She holds up her arm, studies it, looks at me, smiles, and wanders off, never telling me exactly why she stopped by. She climbs into her Plymouth and looks back at William Blott's monument, then drives away like she's in some kind of trance.

B Y TWILIGHT, EVERYTHING'S become faint, all the voices, all the sounds. I can't hear William Blott's trumpet any better if I try. It's like somehow, something's shifted, a zipper that got zipped wrong. It's like I'm hearing them through layers and layers of wool. And I can't tell if they're slipping away or if I am.

I would like to blame it on the storm, but the storm's not here. Not yet. It's beneath me, above me, humming like bees, buzzing before you see them. I'd like to blame it on wind, but there is no wind to speak of. There's just the thickness, dense as a scab. The knowing that the air is wrong, the sky is wrong. There's tension. We're nearing the end of the grace period.

"You cannot stay here," Papa tells me, and I hear him. I hear him, but it's like he's calling from a foreign country, his voice sealed up inside a drum. "You gotta find somewhere else to go."

"I'll be fine," I claim, and I say it too cheerfully—because I don't believe it for a second. I catch myself hollering out over the cemetery, hollering just to trees and stones, and when I look around, it seems so empty. It seems so quiet that I almost panic.

Then Papa shouts back, "You don't understand. This ain't about you. This is bigger. There won't be no way to assure your safety." He spaces between each word like he knows there'll be an echo, a dark shadowing around each syllable, dirt clinging to every sound.

"I'll stay in the house," I compromise. "How big a storm can it be?"

But the Mediator backs Papa up. I can't see her, either, but I can hear her tinkling, then just her voice: "This isn't a request, love. It's an order. I want you out of here before dark. Do you read me?"

"I have a job to do," I call. "Everything I've got's here. I'll be fine here, won't I, Ma?"

But I can't hear anything. I keen my ears. I block out every-thing to hear my ma.

"Ma?"

And there's nothing.

"Ma!" I call. "Ma?"

It feels worse than it did the first time I lost her. I lean against her tombstone and try to imagine it her lap. I close my eyes and make myself pretend that I'm sitting between her legs, leaning up against her, and I breathe and try to imagine her smell, witch hazel sweet.

But my spine finds no comfort against stone.

"Papa?" I cry.

"Get on outta here now," he stammers. "Don't make this harder than it is. Much as we love you, we can't give you what you need."

I get up slow, feeling old in my back and something like wings fluttering inside my chest, like there's something trapped in there, and I can't figure out which direction to walk. A part of me thinks leaving must be the right thing to do—because the graveyard is so different, so lonely, with the Dead calling from a place I cannot reach. But it's *my* place, and all around are the trees and bushes I planted, the bricks I arranged to outline plots, the benches I placed, the fences and gates, the flowers, the fruit dropping down onto graves like blessings. The place is a map, and it's a map of *me*, somehow. To leave it is an impossibility. That's how it seems.

"I ain't going," I say, and I settle over Lucy Armageddon's grave. I reach up and pick a few weeping willow leaves and stick them in my mouth and chew them bitter. At least there is something to taste, something strong.

"Lucy," I call, but I hear nothing. "You gotta tell William Blott that Reba's coming around. You gotta tell him to stop the storm."

I wait for her to respond, but she doesn't.

"Lucy, where are you?" I holler.

"She's here, Finch," the Mediator calls from a low-down place. "But she's busy. We've got work to do that you can't be a part of. You have to go now."

And then I get mad. Because who do they think they are? And how can they just leave me out after all this time? "*Where* do you want me to go?" I ask her. "Where?"

The Mediator returns my tone. "The Holiday Inn, for all I care. Just get out of here. You're not a part of this. It's time to go."

"I ain't going!" I scream to her. "And you tell William Blott that he better get a handle on his rage. 'Cause he's about to punish people he didn't give a fair chance. Reba'd come around if he'd give her time."

If the Mediator hears me, she doesn't let me know. I'd rather she yell back than leave me in silence.

I lean against Lucy's stone and look up at the sky where so much is building. I look out over the land where I have built so much. I wait for the moon, but the moon doesn't come, or the stars—there are no stars.

No moon, no stars, no voices, and the landscape so strange. It's as if I've lost my sisters and brothers.

"I know what it must have been like when you looked in the mirror," I tell Lucy. "When the boy who carved you had gone and you just had those words left. It must have looked so different when he was gone."

I stay out on Lucy's grave for a long time before I see anyone. Then it's a shadow, walking toward me, toting a flashlight, and I know it's Leonard before he even gets close, because he cuts the quiet with his hollering. "Finch? Finch?"

He comes to me at the Lucy stone and says tentatively, "Am I interrupting? You talking with your friend who committed suicide? 'Cause I'll wait—"

And I put my mouth right down to the ground and holler, as loud as I can, "Did you *hear* that?"

"I tried to call," he tells me, offering his hand. "But you didn't answer, and I got worried. I thought you might be out here."

I let him pull me up and walk me back toward the house.

I stop at a boxwood and break off a little branch, the leaves clustered together and wet with leafy rain. "Don't it make you lonely?" I ask him. "To see all those little leaves together and to be so *big*?"

He says, "Not especially, Finch. But I've never seen things the way you do. Come stay at my place, anyway. Just until the storm passes."

"I can't," I tell him. "This is my home. I should be here."

"Just come till the storm's over. Please," he begs. "I could sure use your help. We'll go to the main house to look after Father and Mother until this clears. There are plenty of rooms."

And I think about his father and all the troubles between them. I think about my papa and the last thing he said to me. "I gotta feed the cats," I tell Leonard. "You wanna wait, and I'll follow you?"

ALL MY LIFE, I've seen the Livingston estate, but I've never been on the grounds. The place is huge, with a white picket fence stretched over acres of green fields and trees, and a single gravel driveway points like an arrow to the main house, where the former mayor and his wife still live. It's a white house, with columns in the front, and it looks like a birthday cake to me. It's big, and Leonard tells me it was built before the Civil War. He says it can stand most any storm.

"Is that so?" I ask.

"Well," he says, laughing. "It can stand any *weather*. But Father's nearly brought down the walls a time or two."

Leonard lives in a separate building that he calls "the garage." It used to actually function as a garage before his father closed it in to make a clubhouse for his politician friends. Now the space is an apartment. "A garage apartment," Leonard calls it, though it looks to be bigger than my whole house.

"Nice place," I tell him, and I sit down on an expensive-looking faded couch next to two kittens—the ones he took from my yard—except now they are tame and purring, clean and wearing tiny collars, sleeping on pillows.

"Those are my girls," he says, smiling. "Mary Kate and Ashley."

"You gave them human names?" I say. "I hate it when people do that."

And Leonard just shrugs and grins. "I didn't have time to clean up," he says. "I didn't know I'd have company. Can I get you something to drink?"

"Just water's fine."

I can see his whole kitchen, appliances lined up against one wall, the sink at the very end. He's got bowls stacked up on the counters and boxes of cereal left out on the table, the tops wide open. He opens a cabinet full of cut crystal glasses but brings me my drink in a pink plastic cup that doesn't look especially clean. I think it's probably a compliment—that I'm drinking from a cup he likes. But I can't be sure.

"How long you lived here?"

"Eight or nine years. I didn't move out until I was in my thirties." He laughs.

And it's funny to see him in his space, relaxed. He's taken the chair beside me and kicked off his shoes. His feet carry an odor, but he doesn't seem to notice or mind. It's like being with a whole different Leonard.

All around, there are antique tables that don't match, placed next to a metal filing cabinet, a plastic laundry hamper. He has paisley curtains and a lace tablecloth stained with coffee. There's checked upholstery on the recliner, pushed up beside a floral-print sofa. In one corner, there's a sleigh bed made of cherry, and it's covered in a faded cheap blue comforter with a hole in the shape of an iron. It's the biggest mismatch I've ever seen, and I like it.

"You iron your bedspread?"

"Oh, no," he explains. "I was ironing my pants on the bed when that happened. The phone rang and I forgot—"

And I laugh. "So, did you do the decorating yourself?"

"I hired a professional," he jokes, and gestures with his arms. "Don't you like it?"

"Sure."

"Really, I get all mother's rejects. Every time she goes shopping, I get the hand-me-downs. Lately, she's been buying in bulk. She bought four sets of china in the same year. Keeps forgetting," and he shakes his head. "I've got three of them boxed up in the closet. You need any china?"

"No thank you," I say, wondering what I'd do with china if I had it.

"She gives me all kinds of stuff," he tells me. "This chair was in my bedroom when I was a teenager. Sometimes it's almost like I still live with them."

"You didn't go far. That's for sure."

"Rent's cheap. Besides, with Mother in her decline, there's plenty to do around here."

"You ain't gotta explain it to me," I say. "I lived with Papa till he died." Then I add, "I didn't realize your ma was so sick."

"Physically, she's not too bad, but her mind's going. It's been going on for years, but we didn't notice at first "

"Oh."

"Father has a hard time with it. She says all kinds of things—whatever comes to her mind. Sometimes she talks about when they were young and frisky," he admits, and flushes. "Finch, maybe I shouldn't have brought you here. I just didn't want you to be alone when the weatherman's calling for such bad conditions and the air's so funny."

"It's okay," I say.

"But you see, we'll have to go to the house, and sometimes it's—Hell, Finch, I wish we could just stay here. There's no telling what'll happen. Me and my father . . ."

"I know," I tell him. "Everybody knows. It makes me tired just to think about it."

"I'm sorry," he says, and he stares out the window.

"Come on," I tell him. "We might as well get over there. The wind's picking up." And so we head outside and race across the big yard. The evergreen trees that circle the lawn flap their branches like flags. We crunch along the wet gravel walkway, our faces kept down from the rain.

And I'm hurrying to get inside when Leonard rings the

doorbell. "Don't you have a key?" I ask him. "They're expecting you, right?"

"Yeah," he says, and fishes through his pockets. "If he don't answer in a minute, I'll let us in. Father likes to have control over who comes and goes."

"Jesus," I mutter.

Though in truth, if it wasn't for blowing rain, we wouldn't get wet waiting on the steps. There's an awning overhead to keep us dry, but the wind whisks water everywhere.

Mr. Livingston opens the door slow, like he doesn't care how wet we get. He studies us and seems almost confused.

"Father," Leonard says. "Father, this is Finch Nobles." And he shoves me forward. I stick out my arm, the burned one.

"Well, yes," he says. "We met this morning. It seems like days ago, doesn't it?"

"Yes," I say, and he takes my hand. He pulls me inside and leaves Leonard to deal with the rain and the door.

"I'm glad you could help us out, Miss Nobles. Our regular evening nurse went to be with her family due to the weather."

"Uh, no, Father," Leonard explains. "Finch isn't a nurse. She's here with me, to sit out the storm."

Mr. Livingston looks at Leonard and looks at me, and drops my hand and steps back. Then he steps forward again and says, "I see," in a tone I can't identify. He takes my hand again and says, "My deepest apologies, Miss Nobles."

I look to Leonard because my mind is slow at catching on.

"If you need something done . . ." I offer.

"If you're a guest here, you'll be treated like a guest," Mr. Livingston insists. But the way he looks at Leonard, I know that something's amiss.

We settle down in the study, the chairs all made of leather and big enough for two to sit in. It is hard to imagine Leonard ever living in this house.

"How's Mother?" he asks, and I try to cover the dirt I've tracked in with my shoe.

"Fine. She's sleeping now. I hope she'll sleep out the night."

"I told Finch she could stay in a guest room," Leonard says, but his voice isn't gruff the way I know it to be. His voice is high and he asks it like a question, and I'm suddenly homesick, very homesick, for my little house. All I want is to be sitting on my porch, watching the wind blow. It wouldn't matter if the house blew down with me in it—if I was at home.

Mr. Livingston motions Leonard into the hallway, says, "Excuse us, please, for just a moment," and then I hear the angry whispering, the accusations. I hear Leonard apologizing and Mr. Livingston tapping his foot on the hardwood floor, making quite a racket and whispering loudly about Leonard's mother and what could happen.

And I decide their house is no place for me, storm or no storm. I'd rather be at the Holiday Inn, and though I don't know where one is, I decide I'll find one if I have to, if the Mediator chases me out again.

But when I head for the door, Mr. Livingston suddenly appears and takes my arm. "Allow me to give you a tour, Miss Nobles?"

I look back to Leonard, and he's flushed, his blue eyes wide, his jaw tight. "Go ahead, Finch," he says through gritted teeth. "Father's a real storyteller. You'll enjoy it."

Leonard stays behind as Mr. Livingston leads me around the first floor, giving me the history of the community and of the house as we go. But I can't listen too good for wondering what's going on inside Leonard, and what's going on in the cemetery, and what I'm going to do next.

"This woodstove," Mr. Livingston tells me, "was purchased from a man named Adam Smith by my great-grandfather back in the early 1800s."

"Do you know who made it?" I ask him.

And he looks at me, perturbed. "Who *made* it? I don't care who made it. I care that it's nearly two hundred years old." And he moves us along.

"This moose was shot by my wife's brother, Mr. Albert Dubus. He brought it all the way from Canada . . ."

The head on the wall is dead, of course, but the eyes are wide open, the pelt supple, the rack impressive. And I wish I could talk to the moose. I'd rather talk to the moose than to Mr. Livingston, and after he walks ahead, I reach out and touch its neck.

Mr. Livingston leads me to the kitchen, which is large and well furnished but otherwise unexceptional. "The original kitchen was out back," he says. "If you look out this window, you can see the building right there," and he points and turns on an outside light. "The food was made there, where there was space for a large hearth, and then the servants brought it into the house. But now, with modern appliances"—and he winks—"we don't need such a space."

"What do you use the old kitchen for?"

"Right now, it's not in use," he answers quick. "For many years, my wife, Mrs. Livingston, used the area as a reading room. Before that, it was a play area for the boys—it kept Leonard out from underfoot."

"I see."

"I had another son," he tells me, like I don't know. "God took him from me when he was just a child. He had great promise, that boy. They say he had my eyes."

"I'm sorry," I say. "At least you've got Leonard."

But Mr. Livingston doesn't reply to me at all.

He takes me up the front staircase and shows off the rooms, restored to their pre-Civil War decor. He shows me knickknacks inside each room, clocks and plates and pictures and statues. He shows me gifts he received from important people and points out one particular bed shipped all the way from Switzerland, then points out the place where Leonard cut his teeth. "I had it stripped and sanded and varnished again. But it will never be as valuable," he says.

He leads me to French doors that open onto a balcony. I can see the limbs of trees practicing karate out there. "Children find the one most important thing you own to destroy. You don't have children, do you?"

"No," I say.

"No, I don't suppose you do."

And I don't know what he means by that, but it stings my face. All the doors upstairs are open except for one, and that one, he explains, is his bedroom.

"You can have your pick of rooms, Miss Nobles," he tells me. "And in the morning, if you'll strip the bed of your sheets, I'll have the housekeeper wash them."

Then he takes me down the back staircase. At the bottom, there's a room where Mrs. Livingston is sleeping, just off the kitchen.

"The invalid's room," he says. "We don't want her climbing the stairs."

"Len?" a woman's voice calls. "Is that you, Len?"

"Yes, doll," he answers. "Mildred, we have company."

"We do?" she titters, and I hear feet tapping at the floor.

Then Mr. Livingston does a strange thing. He grabs the doorknob and holds it closed even though his wife works at it from the other side.

"Leonard!" Mr. Livingston calls. "Come escort Miss Nobles back to the study. If you'll wait here—" he says to me, and inches the door just a crack and wedges himself inside "the invalid's room."

I meet Leonard halfway. "I'm leaving," I tell him. "I'm going home."

"Wait," he says. Then he pauses and looks at his shoes. "It was a bad idea, wasn't it? I'm sorry, Finch. I just thought—"

"Just hush," I tell him. I can't hear him apologize again.

I open the front door and stand there, barely making out my pickup across the lawn. I look at Mr. Livingston's truck and Leonard's squad car and think of how I'm going to drive—and where I'll go. The weather's worse already and there's a shutter on a window clanking, a screeching coming from somewhere else. And though the rain comes in, splashing inside, speckling the wooden floor with pinprick dots, I don't close it. The weather's just too bad to leave.

"You mad?" he asks.

"No," I say.

"Why're you mad?"

"I'm not mad," I answer. "I'm uncomfortable."

"Me, too," he tells me. "I thought it'd make it better—for you to be here—but I guess not."

"You shouldn't be uncomfortable here. He's your father, Leonard. Work it out."

"It's not that easy," he says.

"I have easier conversations with my parents and they're *dead*," I tell him. "Why do you let him treat you that way? Either stand up to him or get away from him."

"I just want him to be proud of me," he says.

And that's the last straw for me. "You are *too old* to be acting so childish," I say. "You can't spend your life living for somebody else. And besides that, your father's not going to be proud of you. He's proud of a *moose head*, Leonard. He's proud of the *woodwork*. But you're not an antique, or a limited edition, and you're not imported from a foreign country. He's got more pride in his liquor cabinet than he's got in you."

"That's unfair," he says.

"Hey, I got an idea. Maybe if we took you to a taxidermist and got you stuffed, then he'd be proud. Maybe he could stand you in the corner and hang coats on you, and when guests came, he could say, 'This was my son the policeman. He spent his life trying to make me proud.'"

And as I fuss, the wind picks up. The wind blows so hard that I can't even close the door when I try. It blows so hard that it knocks over the wooden coatrack and peels up the edge of an area rug.

"I wish I could send you *home*," Leonard says, and I can tell I've pissed him off.

"I'm going," I tell him. "I don't want to be here watching you get treated like shit. You can't even stand up for yourself. That's pathetic," I say.

"I know," Leonard says, and he drops his miserable head.

"*No*, you asshole," I tell him. And I get right in his face.

"Don't *let* me talk to you that way! You got to stand up for yourself. Can't you see nobody else is going to?"

"I'm sorry," he says.

"Quit apologizing! You make me sick." I head down the steps, down the walkway, and there's hail now, bouncing on the ground, falling so hard from the sky that it pings on my scalp. And I'm mad at everybody, Leonard included. I'm mad at the Livingstons and the Mediator and Papa and Lucy and especially at the Poet, who I can occasionally glimpse shooting the balls of ice from a BB gun, shooting all around the air.

"Okay," Leonard yells back, and he's chasing me down, right behind me. "You want me to talk hard, I'll talk hard. You're a fine one to be criticizing me, when you've spent your whole life ashamed of your face and running from everybody. You've made it ten times worse for yourself because you never gave anybody a chance, always *expecting* them to mistreat you. You hold grudges like nobody I've ever seen, Finch. Hell, it's taken you this long to forgive me for the first day we started school—and I ain't convinced you've forgiven me now. And that's why you got nobody. I might have a problem standing up for myself, and I might not be worthy of anybody's pride, but I do the best I can, and at least I got some *friends*."

"I got friends," I reply. "Plenty of friends. A *gracious* plenty," I tell him.

"Name them," he says, and he turns me around and starts walking me back toward the house. And I start reeling off people from the cemetery—the same damned ones I'm mad at: "Lucy and William and the Poet and Marcus"—I even say his name, Marcus—"and the Poet and the Mediator and Ma and Papa and Lucy and William and Rulene and Jed." I could go on and on.

"They're all *dead*," Leonard tells me. "You can't exactly call 'em and tell 'em to come pick you up, now, can you?"

"You'd *like* to think that," I say. "You'd like to think it's all in my head, but it ain't, Leonard."

And I think we could go on fighting for hours. I think we could accuse each other and feed off the rain until we wound up nothing but blood and shreds of muscle on the steps. I think we'd enjoy it. Maybe the hail'd beat us to pulp.

But then Mrs. Livingston comes out, in a robe and slippers. Her face has fallen and her hair has grayed, but she still carries a regalness about her. It isn't so hard to imagine her on the steps of the courthouse, baby Marcus in her arms.

"Well, hello," she says to me, and walks right out onto the walkway to touch my cheek, the burned one, stroking her thumb against the burn. "I remember you," she tells me. "You were a member of my childhood class."

And it startles me so much to see her there that way, to feel her touch, that I just say, "No."

"Mother, this is Finch Nobles. She was in school with *me*," Leonard tells her, and he shoves us all back up the steps and inside the door. I drip onto the shiny wood floor.

"No," Mrs. Livingston says. "I remember this face. She's the girl who stole my poodle in New York."

I shake my head.

"Oh yes, you did. That was in 1945, and we were living on Twenty-third Street. And I had the prettiest face in the city and yours was the crudest, of course. So you stole my prancing poodle."

"Darling," Mr. Livingston says, leaning against the mop he's fetched from somewhere, "we never lived in New York. And we never had a poodle."

"Besides that, Finch wasn't even born then," Leonard says.

"What did you do with that poodle?" she asks me. She twists the hem of her robe around and around in her hand while she waits for an answer, lifting it so high that I can see her thin white thighs.

"I fed it painted Easter eggs," I play along. "When it died, I buried it in the yard and grew a poodle tree."

"Oh," she says, delighted, "I have missed you so much," and she comes to hug me.

I don't know how long it's been since I've had arms thrown over my shoulders or a face that I could feel so close to mine. I don't know how long it's been since I've been able to smell someone so clearly, but Mrs. Livingston smells of powder and camphor, and I close my eyes and breathe it in. But she's a short woman, her head resting against my chest, and when I look down, I see that she's staring at me, her eyes blue like Leonard's, a wild dog's eyes.

We're still huddled in the foyer, peering out the door, and Mrs. Livingston says, "This is quite a storm, isn't it? I've never seen such a storm. Did it drop you off here?"

I nod.

"It'll blow out soon and we can all go to bed," Mr. Livingston replies. "Come on in and let's have a beverage."

Leonard offers his mother his arm, and she takes it. I follow behind and take a seat in a rocker.

Mr. Livingston pours clear liquid over ice cubes in thick smoked glasses. When he hands me mine, I take it but don't sip.

"That rocker," Mr. Livingston tells me, "once belonged to a nursemaid from Wales."

"It did not," Mrs. Livingston argues. "It was the rocker I

used to rock Leonard and Marcus." She throws back her drink, swallowing it all in one gulp.

"The two aren't mutually exclusive, my dear."

And Leonard clears his throat.

"You like Dickel?" Mr. Livingston asks me.

"Oh, yes," I reply, though I don't even know what I'm saying or why. I don't know if I like Dickel or not. But the words just come out to join all the other strangeness.

He laughs at me, and I flush, and then the thunder cracks down above the house so hard, it rattles the beams in the floor. Lightning glows at every window, and the lights flicker, flicker, out.

Mrs. Livingston giggles; Mr. Livingston says, "Damn!"

Leonard lights a candle, then another, and he looks at me when he blows out the match.

The house is somehow more tolerable by candlelight, with just shadows and not whole faces. But the wind picks up and it becomes harder to hear each other. The wind screams in the distance.

If I was at home, I would stretch out on the ground and wait for the storm to end. I'd hold myself onto the ground and listen to the earth suck up the rain. And if limbs fell on my back or head, they'd just be like brothers and sisters wrestling and playing acrobat, playing rough. And I wish I could get out there, even in the storm. The ground, the earth, will always hold you, will always hug you back.

"Maybe you should read the Bible to us," Mrs. Livingston says to her husband, her voice suddenly sharp, the giddiness gone. "You used to read the Bible during storms."

"I haven't read the Bible in thirty, forty years—however

many years it's been since Marcus died, that's how long it's been since I've read the Bible. Can you not remember that, Mildred—that I gave up on the Bible when Marcus died?"

"That's true," Leonard agrees.

But I know Leonard would agree with anything his father said.

"Well, that's ridiculous, don't you think?" Mrs. Livingston asks me.

I study Leonard for a clue, but he's stiff, careful, and doesn't look at me, so I just shrug.

"The Lord who took my son will not get my money or my prayers, either one," the old man mutters.

"The Lord didn't take Marcus," Mrs. Livingston tells him matter-of-factly. "I did. I helped him get quiet with a pillow and he never made another sound."

In the silence that follows, I wonder what's more shocking, her murder confession or her tone. We are all stunned, for one reason or another.

"Mother!" Leonard says finally. "That's not true."

"That's *insane!*" Mr. Livingston adds. "Darling, that's not what happened. So *don't say* that. We know what happened to Marcus. He died in his sleep. He simply failed to thrive."

"He was thriving *fine*," she insists. "His *lungs* were certainly thriving." She hops up and pours herself another drink, a bigger one. "You're the one who told me to hush him, Len. You had a speech to make in Richmond the next day. Don't you remember? And you couldn't sleep—"

And I am thankful for the candlelight, for the smallness of it, for the flicker that doesn't make me look at any of them too carefully, for too long. If a crime has happened, I didn't see it. I don't know it. I do not want to know.

"And poor little Leonard," Mrs. Livingston mocks. "He ate until he blew up like a little pig after Marcus died. We took him to a psychologist," she whispers. "He was so nervous, he couldn't help playing with himself."

"Mildred!" Mr. Livingston yells.

"Did I say something *wrong*, Len? Did I say something you didn't *like*?"

"Mother!" Leonard begs.

"It's okay, son," she replies. "Between your brother going away and the little burned child you kept dreaming about . . ."

Then she turns to me, puts her hand over her delicate mouth, says, "Oh, hello," her voice quieter now, her sharpness filed flat.

"Miss Nobles, I am certainly sorry for all this," Mr. Livingston says, rising. "You understand that Mrs. Livingston isn't well. She's suffering a decline and doesn't mean the things she's saying. And now, if you'll excuse us, I think it's time to take her back to bed."

He scuffs across the room, seeming older and less spritely than he was in the morning. But his wife shrinks from him and begins to cry. The closer he gets to her, the more she wails, and when Mr. Livingston reaches out for her, she slaps his hand the way a cat might, if it didn't recognize tenderness, or if tenderness wasn't intended. She bristles, slaps his hand away, and sobs into cushions.

Mr. Livingston stands there, pathetic, calling, "Mildred? Mildred!" He is scared to touch her again.

Leonard says, "Mother? Aren't you tired? Do you want me to help you to bed?" But he keeps his distance, too.

Finally, I go to her, and reach for her arms and pull her up before she has a chance to think about it. "Come on," I tell her.

"Come show me your room," and I lead her there, in the dark, just feeling the walls.

For some reason, all I can think about is what Reba Baker told the newspaper reporter about treating William Blott the way she'd treat Jesus. And even though I'm not too hyped up about Jesus in general, it seems like a good policy, to try and treat everybody good, and it's the only thing I can figure to do with Mrs. Livingston right now.

"I remember you," I tell her. "I remember being little and seeing you at the dedication of the courthouse. That's been a lot of years back. Do you remember that day?"

"Oh yes," she says, sniffling. "I had a new hat. Len brought it to me from Chicago."

"A pink one," I tell her. "And you looked so special that day. I was sitting on my papa's shoulders, watching you, looking at your fancy clothes."

"Will you play with my pretty hair?" she says in a child's voice.

"If you'll come back to bed," I tell her. And I lead her there with my hand on her head, her hair matted in the back. I push her forward.

And I feel my way around "the invalid's room," straightening her sheets and helping her climb in. In the distance, I can hear the wind, howling out, and it sounds like a screaming baby, a screaming trumpet, a screaming woman.

"I didn't *mean* to kill him," she says. "I loved him. He'd just been crying for so long, and I was so tired . . ."

The glass jiggles in the windowpanes, and I wonder if it would matter to baby Marcus if he knew his mother hadn't meant to kill him.

"I think I need to open these windows," I tell her, because I'm scared that the panes might blow out. I pound and pound to get the window up, and once I do, the storm dips inside.

There's a tree just a few feet back, a black cherry tree, and it rains its fruit inside her windowsills. The tree arms beat on the windowpanes like fists, knocking, but like an intruder, not a friend, and I'm not so sure we're in a safe place. I'm thinking we might be better off in a place without so many windows.

I tell Mrs. Livingston that I'll be right back, and I step into the hallway, where I hear Leonard and Mr. Livingston cursing and shouting.

"She did *not* smother that baby," Mr. Livingston bellows. "She's out of her mind."

"We don't know," Leonard insists. "She keeps saying it."

"You are an *insult* to this *name* to even *speak* that way about your mother. You are *no son of mine!*" And then I hear glass breaking and wood splintering, and I run back to Mrs. Livingston.

But the glass and wood were from somewhere else. Not here. Here, Mrs. Livingston kneels at the window, her head stuck out. She holds the window up with her shoulders and catches cherries on her tongue. And she is laughing, deep from her chest.

The lightning pops around us and lights the room in glints, from behind, from the side, from every window, all around. I call to her to come back, but she can't hear me. She's saying something, but I don't know what, in the high, buzzing twirl of screams and hums. There is noise all around, the rushing of a train, and I can only watch from the doorway as the sky lights up and shows a tornado spinning toward us, glowing in lightning like a devil.

And after the lightning, when it is pitch-black again,

the sound getting closer and deafening, I do not go to Mrs. Livingston or try to save her. There's no time. I crouch down in the doorway and wait for the screaming to take me.

Lightning flashes again and there's the sound of shattering, cracking, exploding. There's nothing to see but whirling quickness and a hint of something else, a baby spinning in the mass, leaning out from it to wave, and spinning around again, like a globe, his dark hair flying off like wheat in wind. He darts in and out of the whirling, like a tongue, someone else's tongue, mocking us here in the living world. I think I hear him laugh above the high, whistling roar, but then I close my eyes.

"Marcus," Mrs. Livingston screams. "Mar-cus!"

Then in an instant, so fast that there's no time for surprise, the floorboards explode in one gigantic splintering, and I am hurled into the air, along with the bed and the table and Mrs. Livingston. When I land, I find roots beneath me, the roots of the black cherry tree. I settle with wood against my lower back and no wind in my lungs at all.

And it takes me time to find my air, to make sense of what has happened. I hear bricks tearing apart, scraping against one another, and I think the house is surely crumbling, being lifted away. It isn't until later that I realize that the house has been spared. It's the original kitchen that has disappeared into the night with the baby and the storm, with the sounds of the horn.

"Marcus," Mrs. Livingston screams again. And she pulls herself to her feet and climbs out the window, chasing the storm. But I'm tangled in a tree, still wondering if I'm going to die in the invalid's room.

"Hey, Finch," Leonard yells. "Finch!"

And when I limp out to the other room, I find his father

on the ground, bleeding from the head, where he was hit by a window. And not just the glass. The whole frame.

IT IS TOO late to find her. I know. I want to tell Leonard, "She saw him." I want to tell Leonard, "She recognized Marcus. She was gone from that minute on."

But he can't understand the way death happens slow sometimes. How sometimes people are dead before their hearts stop beating. How sometimes they walk around that way for a long time before their bodies let them go. Sometimes they even have to chase death down.

He can't understand all that. He leaves me there to tend his father, and he says he'll send an ambulance. By the time I get Mr. Livingston bandaged and iced at the place where his head eggs forth, the Vegetable Man has arrived to give us news.

He stomps his boots in the foyer for a solid minute, like mud's worth worrying about when windows and floors explode.

"Who's this hillbilly, and what's he doing here?" Mr. Livingston yells.

And the Vegetable Man pulls off his cap and bows his head.

The Vegetable Man, who got stuck at Glory Road and couldn't get home, says he saw a police car chasing the tornado. "With your wife driving it, Mr. Livingston. Looked to me like she was trying to give that storm a ticket. And it was going over the speed limit for sure," he says. "I thought you ought to know—in case she borrowed Leonard's car without asking."

Mr. Livingston sits, addled, on the floor, saying, "We gotta call the authorities, Miss Nobles. Leonard might need backup."

"We'll do it as soon as we can," I tell him. "The phone lines are down."

The Vegetable Man notices the blood leaking through the bandages I've made by candlelight. He disappears just long enough to find spiderwebs from somewhere; then he spreads them across Mr. Livingston's gashes, to squelch the bleeding, he says.

And then there's Reba Baker banging on the door and whispering to the Vegetable Man, who answers it. She calls me out into the foyer, where she stands with a kerosene lamp and teared-up eyes.

She tells me that Mrs. Livingston didn't make it over the bridge. "She saved our store from destruction, though," Reba says. "And I'll praise God for her forever. That tornado was heading right for us, and I closed my eyes, praying to be spared, and then I heard the siren. She chased that tornado right down the highway, and right over the bridge. But she rammed the car into the steel sides and crumpled it like a tin can. That's what I hear."

"Where's Leonard?"

"He's there, bless his heart. He's waiting for the fire trucks and the wreckers. But there's no need for an ambulance, I'm afraid."

"Go tell the old man," I instruct her. "Don't leave him here by himself, either," and she scowls at me, like I could ever think she'd do something so heartless.

And I run out into the night, and the moon's come out,

mysteriously, along with the stars. I hear a siren in the distance, then see flashing lights headed our way. And then I feel a pain in my backside that I haven't felt before. I put my hand high on my hip and see that I've been scraped raw by tree roots.

"Say there, girlie," the Vegetable Man asks me, "you need a ride to the bridge?"

And I do. Someone has taken my truck—either the tornado or Leonard. I'm guessing the latter, but I don't know how he'd manage to operate it, with the gears the way they are.

The Vegetable Man drives easy, with his high beams on. He drives slow and maneuvers around downed trees, dead cows, pieces of fence and concrete scattered along the road.

"You want a beet?" he asks me, and I say no.

He bites into one laying on his seat.

"Sometimes," he says. "Sometimes these things happen. You can't think about it too hard."

I nod.

"Sometimes something comes along and tears your roots right out the ground, and that's when you know you been planted too long," he says.

I agree.

"Sometimes you been growing one thing in your garden for too many years, and then everything dies. You gotta give the soil time to replenish itself."

"You talking to me in code?" I ask him.

"Shit no," he says. "I'm just talking to pass the time." And he laughs.

A little later, he asks me, "Did that baby you were watching ever cut his teeth?"

"Yeah," I say.

When we get to the bridge, there's just a siren wailing—and I think, at first, that it's coming from the fire truck, but it's not. It's just about all that's left of Leonard's car or his mother, either one, and it doesn't stop sounding for a while. I keep imagining baby Marcus with the siren in his throat.

I tell Leonard I'm sorry. I ask him if he needs me. But he says no, that he'll be okay, that he's headed to the hospital to find his father, that he'll talk with me tomorrow.

"Say, Finch," he says. "I think she might've killed my brother."

"She might have," I tell him. "But that didn't keep her from being a good mother to you." And I don't know why I say such a thing. I don't know if she was a good mother or not.

"Yeah." He laughs, for just a second, before he returns to the scene.

And I just leave him my truck, because what else will he drive? And Leonard's all out of shape, but I've got strong legs. And a couple of miles ain't far to walk after such a big storm—even with a sore backside.

By the time I get to the graveyard, it's nearing daylight, but I don't have the energy for inspections. I see that my house is standing, though most of the roof is gone. I stretch out in bed and close my eyes and shift my legs to make room for a scared cat that I can't even see. I hope it's a cat anyway. I sleep beneath stars, beneath soggy blankets, beneath ivy dangling over my head, and finally, the sun.

I know the Dead haven't disappeared because the sun does rise. The roosters do crow. The clouds move across the sky like always. I know the Dead are around somewhere, but it seems I have gone deaf to them now.

When I rise, I eat my breakfast. I didn't lock the gate, so there's nothing to open. I don't have my truck, and the tractor's turned over, so there's nothing to drive but the lawn mower. I pick up the limbs from the yard and drag them to the edges. Fruits and vegetables splatter against the dirt like they've been dropped from a hundred feet, but my mower is turbo-powered, and so I lift the blade for high grass and I mow. I make applesauce and squashed pears. I mince melons with cucumbers and try not to think about how it's all going to smell in coming days.

I hook a trailer to the lawn mower and head up the hill, stopping to pick up limbs. It's going to be an all-day job. I can tell.

I find tombstones cracked like teeth and part of my fence mangled. And at the top of the hill, I find Reba Baker, scrubbing off William Blott's memorial with ammonia and Tilex.

"I know there's gonna be people coming up here to dig Mildred Livingston's place," she tells me. "I didn't want no remnants of these words left."

"That's kind of you, Reba," I tell her.

"If I had it to do over again, I reckon I'd do it different," she tells me.

"What do you mean?" I ask her.

"I can't abide a queer," she repeats. "I really can't. But I reckon I could have turned my cheek, the way Jesus did, when somebody slapped it."

"Somebody slapped Jesus?" I ask her.

And she looks puzzled, like she's not sure. Then instead of answering me, she says, "Aw, girl," and she stands up and hugs me, and I hug her back before I leave her to her work.

It takes a lot of fixing to get the graveyard back in shape. The adult women's Sunday school class volunteers to help me.

They come out wearing stomping boots and they carry away the random things dropped down on Nobles Hill by the storm: a soggy mattress, a tire iron, a YIELD sign, a toilet seat, a child's plastic horse. There are so many things left behind by the storm, and if any of them have meaning, I can't find it.

One of the women brings along her granddaughter, who I've met before, smoking where she had no business. She hangs back at first, but I shake her hand and she helps me stake off the place where Mrs. Livingston will rest. She holds the string while I tie it to the posts, and I tell her, "Don't never be nobody's project."

And she nods.

T HE BURIAL'S A big one, with the whole town coming out. I stand alongside Leonard, who kneels next to his father, who cries into his handkerchief—and thumbs the baby's stone.

There are hundreds of flower arrangements, from dignitaries and local people alike. And when the burial is over, Leonard stays behind to spread the flowers to other graves.

"Your father's gonna get mad," I tell him.

"My father will get over it," he says. And he's sad, but determined. He's trusting his instincts.

He puts a wreath on William's grave, a basket on the Poet's. A potted plant for Ma, a standing cross for Papa, an arrangement of wood and ribbon for Lucy. He leaves all the roses for his mother but passes a spray of carnations to Marcus. And then there are flowers for others. There seem to be flowers for everyone.

Lois Armour is among the last to leave, staying later than even the fellows who lower the coffin and repack the dirt. She comes to me and says, "I know this ain't a flower, but I was wondering if I could leave it for Lucille."

From her purse, she pulls a crown, tiny and glimmering in her hand.

And I don't know what to say, because there's no way for me to tell whether she's leaving behind the beauty-queen image or keeping it alive in her heart. But she's here, at the graveyard, standing by Lucy's grave.

"I think Lucy'd be glad you came," I say, and I nod when she situates the tiara beneath the stone.

And I don't know if she'll like it or not. I really don't.

"Lucy," she says, smiling. "That's what I called her when she was a baby. The name really suited her better than Lucille, I guess. It didn't sound quite as sophisticated, though."

"How bad was the damage at your place?" I ask her.

"It clipped right by us," she says. "We were so lucky. We didn't lose a shingle."

"I'm happy for you," I tell her. "If you get in the mood to do repairs, you can come help me."

"I will," Lois Armour replies, and she shakes my hand.

I watch her find her car and then drive down the hill. I follow the car with my eyes clear through the cemetery gates.

And then I put Lucy's crown on my head, step up on her stone, and look out from her grave at the world, at all these flowers against the dark branches half-stripped by rain. This cemetery—it's a carnival of color, of life—the trees and bushes hacked up by a storm but still green, the fruits on the dirt instead of on branches, the flowers everywhere, flaunting petals and stems.

In my heart, I know that Ma has lightened, that Lucy's blown her anger out, that Papa's fading, too. I know that things have changed, for better and worse, because they have to. But I'm lonelier than ever, and after all this time, the only truth I claim is this: You can't drag things back from the grave, and trying will just wear you out.

I imagine if I could still go there, if I could haze to the Dead, I'd see a party going on. A good-bye celebration for those who have lightened, the Mediator handing out balloons. I imagine I'd see Lucy dancing, her hair flying wild and her teeth catching light the way jewels do. And William playing happy tunes on a shiny instrument. I imagine I'd hear Marcus chattering and waving, wearing a road map for a diaper and pointing to the sky. And maybe Ma's the one who carries him. Maybe they float on up together, in bubbles Papa blows, with the Poet saying meaningful words and shrugging when everybody claps.

But it's all imagining. I don't really know a thing. And I'm the only one here, with Leonard walking toward the gate now, looking back and stretching out his hand my way, smiling at me 'cause I look silly in this crown. And I don't know how I feel about this place with just me and the broken trees and the river rushing downstream in the distance. In my heart, I know I'm not alone, but I can't be sure—not really. From where I stand, I can't see much, and the only thing that holds me up is my own tough skin and the promise of touch.

About THE AUTHOR

SHERI REYNOLDS is the *New York Times* bestselling author of five novels, including *The Rapture of Canaan*. She lives in Virginia and teaches at Old Dominion University, where she is the Ruth and Perry Morgan Chair of Southern Literature.

Available October 2012

the
HOMESPUN WISDOM
of MYRTLE T. CRIBB

A NOVEL

SHERI REYNOLDS

1

What I did was no more interesting or sinful than this: I took a handful of my husband, Craig's, back pain pills with me when I left that morning for my little operation because I was worried about the potential for pain later in the day. I worried that the doctor might tell me to take ibuprofen—because male doctors often do that to females, refuse to prescribe for them what they'd automatically prescribe for a man; some of them don't even realize they're still blaming Eve—and I didn't want to suffer on my drive back home or into the night. So I took a handful of Craig's medicine as a simple precaution.

My nerves were kinked and frazzled. I'd been up most of the night worrying, and to complicate things more, the fog that morning was so thick you couldn't see, the kind of fog we refer to around here as a malignancy of air. My side mirrors were clouded and wet, and my rearview mirror was broken, so I could barely see to back out of the driveway. Back then I drove Craig's old green truck with the camper top on it. The rearview mirror had been gone for so long that when

Craig had taken the truck in for its yearly inspection, he'd had to bribe the fellow to give us a sticker with some fresh flounder he'd caught that day. So, backing out of the driveway, I rolled down the window, stuck my head out as best as I could, and said a prayer that anything with sense enough to hear the tires crunching on the crushed up clam shells would stay out of my way.

Fog can confuse you because everything looks like an x-ray of itself, recognizable but not reliably so. As I made my way up the road, I gripped the wheel harder than I needed to, feeling not quite like myself. I worried about Craig out there on his boat. The crabbing season had just started up, but how would they even be able to find their crab pots in that weather? Depending on visibility, he might have to come back in, or maybe he was still in the harbor, waiting out the fog. And wouldn't it be just my luck if he decided to swing by the school to bring me flowers (something he's never done) and discover that I'd taken off for the doctor's appointment I'd kept a secret from him?

So I was anxious, naturally, and I caught myself gulping air by accident. I didn't want to have gas by the time I got to the doctor, especially considering the region of my body where he'd be working. That's when I decided to take one of Craig's pain pills—to relax my muscles and calm my nerves, offsetting any potential pain, and also, hopefully, preventing the pootsies.

I don't know if you can blame the drugs for what happened next. My appointment was a two-hour drive away, scheduled for eleven, so I had plenty of time to think. But as I got closer to the doctor's office, the truck started slowing down. It seemed like my foot didn't have the power to push that gas pedal hard enough to get me there on time. I started second-guessing myself, thinking that if I was going to spend my entire secret savings, it should be on something I looked forward to, maybe a trip with my girlfriend Dottie to Atlantic City to play the slot machines or to Pigeon Forge, Tennessee, where Dolly Parton sings.

With Craig's medicine in me, loosening me up, I started wondering if I should be getting my procedure done at all. It was elective surgery and wouldn't have been covered by my insurance even if I'd been fool enough to show them my benefits card. Of course, then the Human Resources supervisor at the elementary school where I work might find out what Craig had been teasing me about for years: I'm lopsided down there, between my legs, with one regular-sized lip and the other one pouting over it. Craig used to make jokes. Sometimes he'd accuse me of attempting to sprout a little ding-a-ling of my own. Sometimes when I'd get out of the shower, he'd point and laugh until I hopped into my panties. "For Lord's sake, baby," he'd say. "Can't you roll that thing up and tuck it somewhere?"

Now where was I supposed to tuck it?

(If it makes you squirm to read this, take a deep breath and hang in there. There are women all over creation ashamed of their bodies, and we need to talk about it more than we do.)

To his credit, Craig always ended such conversations

saying things like, "I'm just messing with you, baby. Don't sulk," or else he'd bring me home a milkshake to make up. But I lived with that kind of teasing day in and day out, and ultimately, it was what drove me toward my spiritual awakening. Right there on that highway headed north, I got just as gnarly-hearted as I could be. What right did Craig have to make me feel bad about my biology? I didn't pick my coochie size any more than I picked my eye color. I got mad with that doctor who'd sworn I'd be happier when I was *symmetrical*, showing me pictures of other women who looked like little girls and making me think I wanted to look that way, too.

And I got aggravated with myself for being suckered by them both. I got so mad that when I stopped to fill up the gas tank, I bought myself a Slurpee—a big one (I wasn't supposed to have anything to eat or drink before my procedure), and I took *another* one of those pills, this time *just because I could*.

I drove right past that doctor's office, blowing the horn and shooting the bird at somebody in the parking lot. (That's not something I'm proud of, and I only tell you this to demonstrate the degree of my frustration. That poor woman was probably there to have her clitoris dehooded, bless her bones.) At that point, I didn't know where I was headed. I just knew that wherever it was, I was going to have my oversized lippy when I got there.

So these were the conditions that led me to the place where I am today, and here are some things to consider, if you ever find yourself in similar straits.

MEATY TIDBITS

Your body isn't a topiary garden. There's nothing wrong with one body part being shaped differently than another. If your husband, wife, or otherwise beloved gives you grief about your symmetry, send that person out into the natural world. Look at the trees growing in your yard or neighborhood. Trees don't grow symmetrically. They stretch and branch and sometimes even contort themselves. The only trees and bushes that look perfectly symmetrical are owned by neurotics with hedge trimmers. These people are akin to plastic surgeons, and you'd do well to stay away from them.

If trees and plants aren't proof enough, have a look at the birds. Go sit on your porch and watch the little finches that make nests in your hanging fern and keep you from being able to take it down when it dies. If you can get a finch to stop hopping around long enough, you'll see that the feathers on either side don't match precisely. Watch the cat, sitting on the mailbox, hoping to grab the finch right out of the fern. The cat has one black paw when all the rest are tabby, and do you think that cat goes around ruminating and bellyaching about it? The cat knows it's perfect as it is. You're also perfect. So before you go looking for someone to balance your breasts, before you wear your hair in a strange configuration to hide your over-large ears, just remember: you could have bigger problems. You could be a finch with asymmetrical feathers, living in a half-dead fern, stalked by a cat with mismatched paws who won't give a fe-fi-fo-fum about your feathers when he crunches down on your tiny bones. Symmetry is overrated. Think about that before you go lopping off your own meaty tidbits.

9 781618 580313